CAPTAIN
HAWKINS

H. Peter Alesso

CAPTAIN HAWKINS

This is a work of fiction. All characters
and events portrayed in this book are
fictional, and any resemblance to real
people or incidents is purely coincidental.

VSL Publications
Pleasanton, CA 94566
www.videosoftwarelab.com

Edition 1.00

ISBN-13: 9781539376361

ISBN-10: 1539376362

Novels by H. Peter Alesso
www.hpeteralesso.com

THE JAMIE HAWKINS SAGA

Captain Hawkins © 2016

THE HENRY GALLANT SAGA

Midshipman Henry Gallant in Space © 2013

Lieutenant Henry Gallant © 2014

Henry Gallant and *Warrior* © 2015

Commander Henry Gallant © 2016

Hope gives some the courage to fight,
but hope is a fragile thing.

1

CALL TO ARMS

The black of night had fallen, but Jamie Hawkins couldn't sleep. Although the surgeons had patched up his many wounds, the remorseless pain persisted, even now, months after his medical discharge from the Marines.

BAM! BAM! BAM!

Hawkins sat up, his heart pounding.

Who could be at the door at this hour?

Not bothering to turn on the lights, he made his way through the darkened country home to the front door, where he found his neighbor, tall scrawny seventeen year old Joshua Morgan, gasping for breath.

"Captain Hawkins, come quick! Come quick, or they'll all be killed!"

"Who? What are you talking about, Joshua?"

"I've just come from the city—it's a war zone. People are dying," Joshua's voice broke. "The hospital is taking care of the wounded and sheltering women and children, but its force shield is buckling." He finished in a breathless rush, "It's only a matter of minutes before it fails."

A troubled frown creased Hawkins's face. Their mothers had been friends and he had known him since Joshua was born.

Has the boy been drawn into the turmoil?

Hawkins had listened to the broadcasts throughout the day, absurd in every detail; the demonstrators declared that they were only protesting injustice, while the government insisted the violence was a last resort against rebels.

Which is the greater lie?

"I told one of the doctors, I knew someone who could help. My flyer's right outside, sir. You must come," begged Joshua, his expressive eyes pleading.

A more sensitive man, who possessed his insight, might have agonized over what was happening in the capital city. Though Hawkins was not unsympathetic, past adversity had left him more hardboiled and cynical than most.

"That's not my concern anymore," he said.

Joshua's desperate voice squealed, "You're a veteran. You could make a difference, sir."

Hawkins put his hands on his hips, threw back his head, and barked, "Ha!"

Then, voicing a deep inner passion, he asked, "What difference can one man make?"

As a Marine, Hawkins had been a hot-blooded warrior, always quick to action, so at this moment of great upheaval, his reluctance to act in the face of frenzied violence surprised him. He ran his hand over the long, jagged scar that marred his chest. One thing was certain, the foolish mutinous passions of the people could only lead to ruin.

But the look that spread across the boy's face was indescribable—it was as if he had just lost his hero.

"All right then, if you won't come, at least tell me how to maintain the shield," said Joshua, with daring and persistence beyond his years. "I'll go back alone, but you must tell me what to do."

"You have no idea what you'd be getting yourself into. All hell has broken loose. Can't you see, you can't contribute anything worthwhile, and most likely something terrible will happen?"

"I must go back! My mother is a volunteer at the hospital," said Joshua, throwing back his shoulders. With a determined jerk of his chin, he challenged Hawkins' gaze, pleading. "Please. Tell me how to fix the shield."

Hawkins opened his mouth, but the words froze on his lips. The boy's courage was a splash of cold water in his face, stinging his sense of honor. It wasn't in his nature to send this boy to certain death—for Joshua could never accomplish what had to be done—nor to let innocents die with the hospital's destruction.

A gritty resolve washed over Hawkins. He said, "Let's go."

Hawkins skillfully maneuvered the single-seat flyer at breakneck speed, his brown leather pilot's jacket flapping behind him. Joshua clung desperately to Hawkins's waist, blinking his eyes against the rain that slashed his face as the motorcycle-like vehicle roared through the dark sky.

Below them Newport was a madhouse—ablaze with scores of savage fires that lit up the horizon. Just hours before, the capital of Jaxon had been a vibrant city, renowned for its culture and history, thriving with business and commerce, home to over a million inhabitants going about their ordinary daily lives. Now it was a battlefield.

Though his home was a mere two dozen kilometers outside the city, several sharp mountain peaks intervened, one tremendous one flanked by two smaller ones, causing Hawkins to race the engine of single-seat turbojet to gain altitude. The engine strained, sputtered, and caught again, its whine rising to a shrill pitch against the altitude as it climbed steeply to three thousand meters.

When they reached the outskirts of the city, they descended to a hundred meters, skyscrapers rose in their path, and without hesitation Hawkins swung the turbojet over a paved highway that connected the suburbs to the planet's capital. The road was choked with traffic— pedestrians, motorcycles, trucks and cars. People of every description swarmed below: disheveled housewives and construction workers, unskilled laborers and local tradesmen, reeking hobos and sharply dressed businessmen, young and old, men and women alike, all seeking safety. Some carried cherished possessions while others brandished antiquated bullet guns; the government had already confiscated most laser and plasma weapons. This teeming mass of human unhappiness snaked along its chosen path intent on escaping the terrifying violence.

Is Joshua's mom in that mob? Hawkins wondered.

Those still in the city suffered under a shower of high-explosive aerial bombs intermixed with artillery shells. As sirens wailed everywhere, Hawkins saw bombers overhead dropping death from the skies and heard almost constant artillery fire in the distance. He couldn't tell who was doing the shooting.

After his initial reluctance to come, now that he was here Hawkins agonized over whether he would be too late. A nearly impenetrable wall of smoke, flame, debris, and explosions forced them to a crawl, adding heart-wrenching minutes to their journey.

Every few minutes another wave of jets roared overhead and a new barrage of artillery shells rocked the city. The raging fires pulsed, like the blind fury of an agitated beehive. Small fires exploded into big ones right before his eyes. Big ones dwindled under the valor of firemen, only to flare up again a few moments later.

The city's civil-defense shelters already overflowed with refugees. Many citizens had left their homes, defying the flames to run to bomb shelters throughout the city, only to find there was no room for them. In addition to widespread death and injury, everywhere Hawkins saw evidence of psychological trauma—children sat in rubble next to their dead parent's bodies, adults wandered aimlessly, dazed and bleeding. With panic spreading and raw nerves eroding by the minute, it was impossible to gauge how much more the citizens could take. The people prayed for a respite—but they had little hope for mercy on this night.

Hawkins heard the crackling of the closest flames and the screams of both victims and firemen. Smoke blurred his vision and seared his lungs. Nevertheless, he kept going with Joshua clinging to his waist.

"Ack! Ack!" Joshua choked on the acrid air.

"Here cover your mouth with this handkerchief," yelled Hawkins over the uproar.

EEEEEEERRRRR!!!

The sirens wailed.

Hawkins cursed.

"Oh, no," said Joshua. "Are we too late?"

"We're almost there," said Hawkins.

Detonations overhead shook the buildings around them. The sky was alive with a deadly dance of destruction.

BOOM!

Then another—

BOOM!

This time the explosion sent shrapnel hurtling into the flyer and its occupants. The engine sputtered and died, and Hawkins needed every bit of his piloting skill to make a controlled crash landing between two burned-out buildings. As they struggled to disentangle themselves from the mangled flyer, flames surged from the engine. Scrambling to their feet, Hawkins and Joshua were barely half a dozen meters away before it exploded.

Despite their cuts and burns, they set out on foot for the hospital, braving the misery of suffocating black smoke, scorching heat, and particle dust that swirled around them.

They felt as if they had stepped onto another world. The greatest fires were directly in front of them, whipping hundreds of feet into the air. Smoke ballooned up in great clouds. Desperate people pressed against the entrance to a nearby shelter—safety lay on the other side. A uniformed guard barked uselessly through a megaphone, "Remain calm! Don't push!"

Farther down the street, Hawkins watched soldiers break through the defensive ring of some diehard demonstrators, sending them fleeing in every direction. He couldn't quite make out the shouted invective, but he could read one oversized banner as it fell:

"Beware the Wrath to Come!"

EEEEEEERRRRR!!!

Windows rattled as an artillery shell exploded nearby, scattering what remained of the crowd.

Finally, Hawkins and Joshua reached the hospital entrance. Black curtains were drawn across the windows to keep shattered glass from sending shards into the street.

As they ran toward the building, they saw the hospital's shield collapse while a barrage 'walked' its way directly toward them. The nearby shells were distinct and sharp, while those far away were soft and muffled. The ground shook under their feet.

They ran into the hospital main entrance.

They dashed through the door. An excitement—not fear, not horror, but rather awe—swept over Hawkins. Lining the hospital's corridors were groups of wounded, terror-stricken fugitives from the battle, as well as innocent civilian victims of the indiscriminate explosions. Only a few nurses tended to the injured in the aisles. He saw parents trying to reassure their frightened children. One mother held a screaming baby in her arms while her other children whimpered, clutching at her skirt.

Where will this trail of suffering end?

He didn't recognize any of the many faces he passed, but hands stretched out, grasping at him, imploring him for help.

On nurse asked, "Please, will you help me move these patients out of the corridors?"

He shook his head, mumbling as he raced past, "I've got a vital job to do, but I'll come back."

He made his way through the hospital toward the power generator and force shield control center in the basement of the facility. Several inches of water covered the basement floor, one electric outlet was shooting sparks, most of the lights were out, and the few remaining ones flickered.

Sloshing through the dim corridor, Hawkins ran smack into a slender young brunette in surgical garb. She gaped in shock as the apparition emerged from the chaos. In his pilot jacket, tanned rawhide trousers, and knee-high leather boots, he looked like a dashing swashbuckler of olden days—not at all what she was expecting.

When she saw Joshua behind him, she recovered her wits and gasped, "Thank goodness Joshua brought you. I'm Alyssa Palmer. I was beginning to despair that help would ever come."

Hawkins said, "Doctor, I need access to the power control room to restore the force shield. Can you get me through the security locks?"

A minute later, she punched her security code into the access pad on the heavy security door to the control center.

Since the shield had already collapsed, the hospital was dangerously exposed and every minute counted. Despite the heavy weight of responsibility, Hawkins's mind was already processing a plan.

Hurry!

Fortunately the hospital shield was similar to combat force fields he had trained on. His eyes scanned the equipment, assessing and diagnosing the damage to the deflector field. Quickly recognizing the lack of parts and tools at hand, he sent Joshua to get them from an ancillary supply room. After what seemed an eternity, Joshua returned and Hawkins set to work. Before long, backup power generator coughed, then caught and purred contentedly.

When the shield indicator flickered to life, Alyssa's eyes lit up as well. Her hands gripped Hawkins's arms and she said, "Thank you. *Thank you.*"

With relief, she returned her attention to the many injured victims in desperate need.

With the shield once again protecting the hospital, its inhabitants had a moment of reprieve, even while the city continued to cry out in pain.

After setting the shield controls to automatic, Hawkins returned to help. He moved patients from the corridor for the harried nurse. He found Joshua consoling his mother in a waiting room. Not wishing to intrude, he wandered around the hospital until he walked into the main triage clinic, a large room boasting ultramodern diagnostic, monitoring, and regeneration equipment.

He watched one patient being lowered into a regeneration chamber, very much like the one he had spent considerable time in the previous year. An oxygen mask was placed over the patient's mouth and nose. Tubes in the veins allowed chemicals and nanobots to be pumped throughout the cardiovascular and endocrine systems. The nanobots handled preprogrammed internal microsurgery and cell repair throughout the body. Electrical sensors wired into the spinal column controlled the brain and nerve functions, while others monitored heart and lungs. Under AI control, organs and nerve function could recover from even severe trauma.

Across the room, he saw Alyssa caring for a young girl. He sat down quietly on a chair in the corner and watched.

The child's tears streaked down her cheeks. A significant part of her body showed severe burns, and a deep gash on her leg bled freely.

Alyssa said, "Don't be afraid. It's going to be all right. I'm going to make the pain go away and fix your leg, good as new."

Her gentle, soothing touch calmed and reassured the child despite the tubes and wires attached to her body.

Alyssa said, "A little stick," and with a sonic needle she injected local analgesic into the burn and wound areas. A laser scalpel cut away the burned tissue. She dabbed a healing gel over the burn area. Hawkins recognized the medical patch from a soldier's battlefield kit; it helped to relieve pain and promote healing. Finally, with a few rapid motions, she deftly sutured the wound. Throughout the procedures, she spoke in a soft voice to distract the girl.

"My parents were both physicians. I used to sit in the corner of their clinic—just like that man," she said, nodding at Hawkins.

"I watched them perform minor miracles through modern medicine. It was then that I made up my mind to be a doctor, like them, so that I could take care of little ones," she said, smiling and poking the child in the chest, "just like you."

Before the girl knew it, the ordeal was all over. As Alyssa put the final touches on her bandage, the tears stopped and her frown turned into a smile.

"Thank you," said the child, hugging Alyssa around the neck.

"Nurse," called Alyssa. A nurse came and led the child back to her anxious parents, who had been waiting nervously outside the room.

She watched the child leave and sighed, "They're gone now—my parents."

Hawkins nodded sympathetically and said, "I lost my parents early, as well."

"You might as well let me clean up those gashes and burns." Alyssa pointed to the large bloodstains on his jacket and trousers.

"They're nothing. They can wait. I'm sure there are many others in greater need," he said crossing his arms and tucking his hands in.

"Actually, they look more serious than you think. Better let me treat them." She smiled impishly and said, "Don't be afraid. It's going to be all right. I'm going to make the pain go away and fix your leg, good as new."

A crooked smile slowly formed on his lips. He said, "As you say."

She moved so quickly and efficiently, that he found his outer clothes removed and a plasma drip in his arm in nothing flat. She applied local analgesic and antiseptic while suturing a dozen wounds, several of them substantial.

"Oww!" escaped his lips only once while she stitched a twelve centimeter gash in his calf.

"Oh, that didn't hurt," she mocked.

"No, of course not," he said, clenching his hands tighter as he looked around to see if anyone had heard. But with so much else going on in the emergency room, no one paid him any attention.

She said, "You look like a man of action, but Joshua said you were uninvolved in what's going on."

"What is going on? Can you explain it me? It all seems rather jumbled," grumbled Hawkins.

She gazed at him and blinked in surprise. "Joshua said you were a Marine."

"*Were.* I was medically discharged last year." A frown darkened his face.

"That would explain all this scar tissue," she said, examining his torso.

"Huh," he grunted.

"You fought against Hellion?" she said smearing a healing gel to a second degree burn on his arm.

"Yes. And that war grinds on remorselessly, apparently endlessly, even without me."

"You don't seem like someone who would be content to remain on the sidelines during times of trouble."

"Times of trouble?" he said, raising his eyebrows in mock jest.

"Our city is in ruin because the demonstrators believe our democracy is disintegrating. They claim President Victor is corrupt, eroding basic freedoms with the intent to establish a dictatorship."

"And Victor has exclaimed, with equal vigor, that the protestors are proxies for Hellion, determined to bring down the administration and pave the way for an invasion," responded Hawkins.

"Well, which do you believe?" she asked.

"You mean which is the greater lie?"

"Yes. Which?"

"How am I to know?" he said, throwing up his hands. "Remember, I am...*was*...a Marine, and that leaves an indelible mark. So despite the egregious outpouring of suffering and turmoil, I've witnessed, I am not inclined to lend my combat skills to the hopelessly dysfunctional cause of the rebels."

Alyssa put the final touches on his bandages and said, "All done. You can get dressed now. I have other patients who need my help." Poking him in the chest, she added, "just like you."

She was gone in an instant.

Suddenly alone, Hawkins felt unsettled, as if her leaving tore away something he desperately needed.

Beyond the hospital shield's protection, incendiary bombs continued to fall. Frequent pinpoints of dazzling white lit up the hospital interior, illuminating the suffering victims as each bomb exploded. They went out one by one, as the unseen firemen smothered them with fire retardant, but as soon they eliminated one, another building was on fire.

With the coming of dawn, the bombs and shells finally stopped. The earth-shaking explosions ceased; the suppressed fires stayed out. The lull indicated, Hawkins speculated, that the Jaxon military had regained control of the city and put an end to the uprising. Or as the government proclaimed, it had successfully crushed a rebellion.

As the city quieted, the military and police swarmed the area, demanding that the hospital shield be lowered.

When Hawkins complied with the authorities, rough hands seized him. They dragged him away from the shield control panel and pushed him, along with the rest of the hospital staff, into the entrance corridor.

The senior officer shouted, "Take these rebels out, and shoot them.

2

ONLY THE BRAVE

After twenty-four hours of non-stop brutal violence and cruel bloodshed, the soldiers had had no sleep and little food or water. They had repeatedly engaged in hand-to-hand combat against the demonstrators. Even though the soldiers were heavily armed and armored, they had taken serious casualties. Now, tired and angry, everyone they found looked like a rebel.

The hospital had been a place of healing—now it became a makeshift prison. In a large observation room, the soldiers sorted people into three groups: the wounded men, a smaller group of women and children, and the medical personnel including Hawkins and Joshua.

With bloodthirsty eagerness, the ranking officer repeated, "Take these rebels out and shoot them," pointing to the first group.

As the first group was headed toward the door, Hawkins stepped forward, planted his feet wide apart, and shouted, "Stop, Colonel!"

Outraged at the ruthlessness of the order, he put his hands on his hips and said, "You can't execute these men."

The officer turned toward the disturbance and said harshly, "It is my duty to safeguard the nation. Am I to care for the lives of rebels?"

"For the sake of humanity, yes," said Hawkins, his voice strong and vibrant. With an unyielding stare, he added, "This is still a civilized world, not a lawless state."

Crossing his arms without taking his eyes off the interloper, the immaculately attired colonel seemed disconcerted.

Hawkins said, "These men have not been properly charged."

The colonel remained unimpressed.

"There are always witnesses to any massacre, Colonel." Making a grand sweeping gesture with his arms, he added, "Just look around."

The colonel frowned as he surveyed the frightened faces of the women and children. Then seeing the uncertainty on the faces of his own men, his frown deepened into an angry scowl.

"Eventually, there'll be a reckoning," said Hawkins, waving his hand to take in the hellish carnage throughout the city. "The government will look for scapegoats to justify this harsh reality. It wouldn't be prudent to be so easily identified with merciless acts."

The colonel stared daggers at Hawkins. For a moment his hand hovered over his pistol, as if he were considering putting a bullet in Hawkins's head right then. Instead, his eyes narrowed as recognition dawned on his face. He sneered, "Why, I know you. I served with you at Gambaro Ridge." A smile crept across his face and he said with a strange blend of sarcasm and irony, "You were killed."

"Not quite," responded Hawkins with an outlandish grin.

"I saw you shot to pieces when you recklessly charged the enemy stronghold," said the colonel, smirking, and nodding his head. He laughed, "That was insane. You were definitely killed."

"As you say," said Hawkins, letting a chortle escape his lips.

"Your assault gave the rest of us a chance to escape," the colonel remarked thoughtfully, considering the memory in a new light.

Undecided on how to deal with such an uncommon man, the colonel pointed at him and exclaimed to his troops, "Ha! Here's something you rarely see—a disgruntled ex-Marine."

A roar of laughter erupted from his soldiers.

Hawkins threw his head back and laughed as well, "Ha!"

The colonel stepped closer to inspect him.

A small, jagged scar over his right brow was nearly hidden behind the shock of unkempt sandy brown hair, which draped over his forehead in a careless manner. He was tall with an athletic build, and he stood forward on balls of feet, like a boxer. His strong jaw and intense gray-blue eyes purported an iron will. The colonel remembered Hawkins as a courageous, but utterly reckless, officer.

Hawkins recognized the colonel as well. Anthony Rodríguez was swarthy, ruggedly handsome with a broad mustache and a muscular physique. Hawkins remembered him as a fashionable man, his uniform always well-tailored. What he lacked in imagination, Rodríguez made up for as a stickler for protocol, meticulously carrying out orders in order to further his career.

After a long moment, Rodríguez barked, "Don't be foolish enough to believe I feel any obligation to you. You did your job. Now I'm doing mine."

Throughout the observation room, frightened people waited for the tension to burst. They realized that in many ways their fate was bound together with this tête-à-tête.

Rodríguez said, "I don't believe your battlefield antics were ever acknowledged. Some might have thought you a fool."

Stone faced, Hawkins retorted, "Then you stand here today—alive—as a testament to my folly."

Coloring slightly, Rodríguez took a moment to recall his orders and began parsing the words to extract their broader intent. Finally, he asked, "What are you doing here? Are you a rebel?"

"I'm no rebel," said Hawkins adamantly. "The genera- tors were failing. No technicians were left to bring up the backups, so I was called here to protect the women and children."

"Called here? By whom?"

"What does that matter?" asked Hawkins.

"I'll decide what's important," Rodríguez snapped.

Joshua spoke up, "It was me."

"What was your business here?"

"I came to help."

"Help whom? Were you with the demonstrators?"

"Yes, but I was looking for my mother . . ."

"There. By his own admission, he's a member of the rebels," said the colonel delighted, at finding something clearly within the bounds of his orders.

Joshua tried to explain, "I not a rebel. I just wanted to …"

Rodríguez ordered, "Put him with the rest of the rebels."

As the soldiers pulled Joshua away and placed him with the group of rebels, Hawkins said, "He's just a boy. He was involved in things beyond his understanding."

Rodríguez shot a disdainful look at Hawkins and asked, "Oh! Were things beyond YOUR understanding, when you aided the rebels hiding in this building?"

"I came to succor the weak and helpless, as is the duty of any man of honor," said Hawkins.

Offended and enraged, Rodríguez stormed, "No! You were aiding a rebel force attacking our nation's capital."

"I—was—saving—lives," spat Hawkins. "Once again!"

The veiled reference to Gambaro Ridge made Rodríguez flushed crimson—the emotional cocktail of anger and humiliation was so powerful that his face looked as if it would explode. His voice contorted into a rapid-fire staccato of orders, "Place this man under arrest—along with the rest of these rebels—march them all to prison."

Several pairs of hands reached out and grabbed Hawkins, but as he twisted free several more soldiers joined in the brawl. Six soldiers were as battered and bruised as Hawkins before they managed to pin him down. They bound his wrists and flung him against the wall with the rebels.

His dark eyes blazing with contempt, Hawkins's deep voice boomed, "Anthony Rodríguez, if I survive this barbarity," he took a deep breath, and said slowly, "I hope to chance upon you—once again."

Other distraught prisoners began yelling their own protestations, but Rodríguez bellowed over the clamor, "Take them away! Take them away!"

3

TAINTED VERDICT

With his flowing ruffled black robe draped around him, the frail wizened sour faced Senior Justice Alfred Augustus Richter gazed at the innocuous prisoner, unaware that he was holding court on someone unusual—never mind extraordinary. The indictment on the table before him was flush with red marks, official seals, and high-ranking signatures. Tags and attachments cluttered the dog-eared pages. Richter surmised that this case had garnered a great deal of interest from some lofty individuals. He had never seen such a harsh and disparaging document in his thirty years as a judge. Perhaps the circumstances were not as clear-cut as he imagined.

From the court bench several meters above the prisoner's head, the senior justice squinted to bring Hawkins into sharper focus. Despite the shaggy hair that flopped over his brow, he looked more soldier than rebel with his military bearing and a firm, square jaw that declared, "I am unafraid." Yet he kept shifting his weight from one foot to the other, undermining the look of unwavering calm—as if fluctuating between confidence and unease…or was it possible he was in pain?

Dressed in an orange prison jumpsuit that covered his ragged and stained bandages, Hawkins stood alone as the focal point of the room with a single chair behind him. He had no lawyer for his defense. The high court bench loomed over him at the front of the room while the empty jury's box was set off to the left side of the room. The prosecutor sat at a table on the right, methodically sorting through a pile of documents. Security guards stood at every corner of the room. In the back, citizens packed the rows of audience seats, whispering, their curiosity focused on Hawkins, as if he were the tip of a judicial iceberg.

The unique, ultramodern architecture of the Newport courthouse, with its arched ceilings and high glass panels, gave the building the look of a major corporate office rather than the most important judicial building on the planet. However, on this gloomy day, only a few faint rays of sunshine filtered through the overcast clouds to cast a cobweb-like net at Hawkins's feet.

Stretching his wizened face with his best sarcastic smile, Richter glanced down at Hawkins, and asked, "I hope you don't mind my asking you a few questions before the formal proceedings start?"

It was unusual for him to directly question a prisoner in his court, especially given such a comprehensive indictment. In fact, he couldn't remember ever having done it before. He ordinarily left the job of eliciting testimony to the prosecutor, but this case had aroused his curiosity. He looked again at the thick documents on the table—rife with brash accusations, startling declarations, and ugly notations that attempted to bridge the gap between ludicrous insinuation and actual evidence.

"No...no, not at all," said Hawkins, his indifferent words belying the fulsome gesture of his hands.

Richter recalled the stories he had heard about the former Marine. It didn't seem likely that this brash young man had committed all the crimes he was accused of— after all, the prosecution had no physical proof of rebel activity—and yet Richter was reluctant to let the possibility melt away. Considerable political interests were at work here, with specific motives that were unknown to him. A judge was, after all, a political animal, and he lived in a time where his superiors frequently second-guessed motives and actions. What if this disheveled individual actually had committed all these treasonous acts? What would Richter's fate be if he mishandled the trial?

"You are an exuberant prisoner. I'm reminded of some brigands I've sentenced."

"I can only speak for myself."

"Not according to your accusers. They say you were only too eager to speak for others without being asked," said Richter, waving the indictment in Hawkins's face. "Just look at these red marks and condemnations, many from prominent leaders in our government."

Richter savored the deflated look on Hawkins's face; the determined expression flagged as if he had been punched in the gut. Having extracted a full measure of discomfort, and thereby established his authority, Richter shifted this tactics, "I'm really enthusiastic about hearing your defense."

"You…you will hear me?"

Richter said, "Of course, there may be considerable controversy, but then again, controversy makes for stimulating discourse. I expect a great deal of attention will be drawn to this matter and justice must not only be just, but also *be seen* to be just."

Hawkins gave a harsh laugh. "Ha! Senior Justice, you've made a damn brilliant decision."

While Richter's words sounded sincere, the judge was enjoying his game of cat-'n-mouse. A slick smile crossed his otherwise stately countenance. "Fine. Now at the risk of being indelicate, let me start by asking—are you guilty of treason?"

"I shall be equally indelicate in my reply," said Hawkins. He dropped his hands to the table, leaned forward, and professed loudly, "No! These allegations are all damnable lies."

The spectators exploded with excited babble.

"Order! Order!" demanded the judge pounding his gavel.

He waited until the crowd became quiet once more. Then he admonished the accused, "You will not address this court so impudently, sir."

Hawkins nodded silently.

"You are in a court of law and you must comply with the Rule of Law," said the magistrate from his lofty perch. "You must answer guilty, or not guilty."

"I beg Your Honor's pardon—not guilty," said Hawkins, sounding contrite, but looking not the least repentant.

The Senior Justice leaned back in his chair, solemn and composed. He said, "Then, in your own words, tell this court how you came to be in this predicament."

Hawkins took a deep breath and plunged into his version of the dramatic events that night.

The judge let him speak for less than a minute before interrupting impatiently, "I've heard enough. Mr. Prosecutor, bring in the jury and present your case."

Murmuring filled the courtroom as the jury filed in. The jurors looked inquisitively at the defendant while the oath was administered and the indictment was read.

The prosecutor had a small pointed nose with wispy whiskers beneath it. He stood up and held his hands close to his chest with his head tilted to one side when he addressed the court. While his appearance was slight, his speech was flamboyant. He spoke out of the corner of his mouth as he denounced Hawkins as a traitor and added a litany of other equally scurrilous labels for good measure.

Colonel Rodríguez was called as the only witness for the prosecution. Never once looking directly at Hawkins, he described the hospital and its inhabitants as he found them that night. He testified that Hawkins had restored the shield that sheltered the band of rebels from his soldiers, acknowledging that Hawkins lowered the shield when ordered. Rodríguez made no mention of his original order to execute the prisoners.

The judge asked, "Do you dispute the direct testimony of this witness?"

"The events that Colonel Rodríguez described are factual," said Hawkins, stone faced.

"I am glad you chose to admit your complicity without equivocation. We shall reach the truth all the sooner," the judge grinned broadly. "Do you have any questions you wish to put forward to the witness?"

"Yes, Your Honor, I do" said Hawkins getting up and taking a step toward the witness chair. "Colonel, what would have happened to the innocent women and children seeking shelter in the hospital if the shield had not been restored during the bombardment?"

"Don't answer that, Colonel," the judge interjected. "Mr. Hawkins, you are not on trial for any action you undertook to hurt, or help, any bystanders in the hospital. Their disposition is immaterial to this court." Richter paused while he placed his hand on the red-marked, dog-eared, multi-tagged indictment document and slid it to the side of his desk. Then he said, "You must confine your questions to the germane issue of the court—did you actively aid members of a military group undertaking to overthrow the Jaxon government. Any diversion from this topic will be stricken from the record. Don't waste the court's time with any further allusion to anyone other than the rebels in the hospital. Do I make myself clear?"

Hawkins blanched.

"I would have the members of jury hear my defense," Hawkins said desperately.

Again a murmur was heard in the court.

"Silence! Any further disturbance will result in my clearing the court," shouted the judge.

Then turning back Hawkins, he rasped, "You shall have your say in good time, rascal."

The judge glared at Hawkins. "Colonel Rodríguez, you are dismissed."

Without further interruption, the prosecutor gave a short speech on the treasonable act the defendant had committed. When the defamation was complete, the judge allowed Hawkins to conduct his own defense, such as it was.

The only defense witness, he was allowed, was Joshua Morgan.

Joshua shifted uneasily in the witness chair, tugging at the collar of his orange jumpsuit. He looked scared, but otherwise appeared unhurt.

Hawkins asked him to describe what they had done at the hospital. Joshua explained how they had worked together to restore the force shield.

"Joshua Morgan, you were a neighbor of Mr. Hawkins?" interjected the prosecutor with the judge's permission.

Joshua cast a troubled gaze at Hawkins.

The prosecutor waited a moment, then pressed, "Is that right?"

Joshua asked "Is what right?"

"Joshua Morgan, were you the defendant's neighbor on the day in question?"

"I was, but I kind of left that day."

"Come, come, man, you're obfuscating the truth."

"I can't say that."

"Why is that?"

"I don't know what that word means."

There was a titter in the courtroom.

The prosecutor peppered Joshua with questions until he admitted both that he was in the demonstrations and that wounded demonstrators were being treated in the hospital.

"But there were women and children, as well," exclaimed Joshua, trying to redeem his testimony

"Strike that," intervened the judge. "The witness will confine himself to answering questions and not contribute his own musings."

The judge gave Hawkins an opportunity to question Joshua, but again disallowed any mention of the women and children in the hospital.

Hawkins objected, "Your Honor, I had hoped for justice. At the least, I expected a fair hearing, but this trial is a travesty. I have had no opportunity to examine the evidence against me, nor been allowed to call further witnesses in my defense."

Some of the spectators, who might have been government officials or reporters, snickered and made disruptive noises.

The Senior Justice pounded his gavel again and again, "Enough! I will not tolerate such outbursts."

Turning to Hawkins, he said, "Rogue! I will not allow slanderous remarks to be made against this court. Do you seek to waste the court's time with endless subterfuge? You have had every reasonable opportunity to defend yourself, but your only defense is to proclaim yourself innocently caught up in the vortex of war, despite testimony to the contrary. Evidence presented here in this court has established that you willingly aided rebels. I shall not waste this court's time with any further nonsense from a villainous traitor, the likes of you."

Hawkins looked as if he wanted to say more, but again the senior justice gaveled for silence and said, "Speak out of turn again and I shall have you gagged."

A string of foul curses exploded from the defendant's mouth, excoriating the Senior Justice and his supposed 'Rule of Law.'

The judge waved to the security guards, who seized, bound, and gagged Hawkins, tossing him back in his chair.

Looking expectantly at the jurors, the prosecutor summed up his final arguments to the court. He addressed himself to the jury, not the crowd, gauging whether they were sympathetic to his words.

"Certain treasonous acts cannot be denied. While some actions may be subject to multiple interpretations, the defendant's actual rebellious activities are not in dispute," said the prosecutor pointing a finger directly at Hawkins.

He concluded, "You've heard the evidence in this case. It is now your solemn duty to bring in a verdict of guilty in this matter."

"Now then," said Senior Justice Richter, at last satisfied. "The jury will withdraw and reach the only verdict possible in the case of the Jaxon government verses the treacherous rebel, Jamie Hawkins."

Several of the jurors rose, but the jury foreman spoke up immediately, "Your Honor, there is no need for an adjournment. We are ready to render our verdict."

The jurors looked at one another and nodded. The foreman said, "Guilty."

The smile on the senior justice's face expanded even more. He banged his gavel and said with satisfaction, "This court sentences Jamie Hawkins to life imprisonment at hard labor in the Zeno Penal Colony."

4

FAR AWAY

Hawkins recalled the orchid in his backyard and the rich ripe peaches dripping juices with each bite, of the fruit pies his mother had baked and set on the window sill to cool, of the sweet pungent scents that drifted past his nostrils, of the warm spring breezes when he would sit on the front stoop eating those pastries. For a time he was able to cloak himself within the sensory extravaganza of those memories, but soon, against his will, the repulsive nauseating stench of close quarters and deplorable sanitary conditions permeating the transport vessel pulled him back to reality, causing him to nearly retch.

Midway through the two month voyage to Zeno, within the confines of the overcrowded cargo bay, Hawkins was lost in the crush of assorted crooks, hardened criminals, and murderers, along with those the Jaxon government found equally repugnant—rebels—every man jack of whom was condemned to a life sentenced.

He picked up a cup of brackish brown-tinted water and grimaced as he took a swallow, but the fowl taste forced him to spit it out. He unenthusiastically chewed on a moldy bit of synthetic nutrition bar that served as his daily ration, but the decade-old substance, probably from a military field kit, had deteriorated beyond palatable. Resigning himself to the necessity of consuming some sustenance, he swallowed the portion whole and trusted his stomach to somehow digest the distasteful lump.

Rising from his uncomfortable metal seat, he pushed his way through the cargo bay, shoving past surly, scowling men until he reached one of the few ventilation grills that admitted a faint whiff of fresh air.

"Let me by," he said, pressing forward insistently.

"Hey, look out," one beefy man protested. He turned to shove back, but after sizing Hawkins up, let him pass.

Hawkins finally reached the handrail that ran up the side of the bulkhead and pulled himself up, hand over hand, until he reached a tiny viewport ten meters off the deck. Originally intended for use by ship workers when they moved cargo, the port now served as the only outside view available for any prisoner vigorous enough to climb up to it.

Hawkins glanced down at the oppressively claustrophobic space, then with relief, shifted his gaze out the viewport at the void beyond.

The Jaxon star system consisted of six planets, separated down the middle by an asteroid belt. The three inner planets were united as a democracy governed from the second planet, also named Jaxon. On the other side of the asteroid belt, the three remaining planets were under the thumb of dictatorship, ruled from the fifth planet, Hellion. Through the centuries, up to and including the Twenty-Third, communication and travel between stars remained challenging. The vast interstellar distances left the Earth colonies mostly on their own. The earth-like planets had been settled quickly, while the less hospitable ones had been terraformed more slowly. It had been five decades since a ship from another star had visited Jaxon and during that time, Hellion had started a war.

As the star field blinked against the inky black vacuum, Hawkins tried without success to pick out Sol—lost among the bright points of light, billions of kilometers away.

He shook his head.

Damn.

At last, the cargo ship arrived at the star system's third planet, Zeno, at the edge of the asteroid belt. For days, rumors had circulated among the prisoners that they would make landfall, but none had truly believed it until the derelict vessel dropped into orbit and they got their first glimpse of their new home. They disgorged by the score as shuttlecraft moved back and forth from the vessel to the spaceport. The astonishing human wrecks that flooded into port shocked even the most coldhearted guards. The red-rimmed eyed beggars were desperate for decent food and medical attention. After being confined in the cargo bay in unsanitary conditions, malnourished, and given foul water, disease had spread amongst them causing dozens of deaths. Hundreds of pathetic souls no longer could claim to be part of civilization after the squalor they had endured aboard the transport where they had been treated more like merchandise than human beings. Many had once been part of an inspired host, marching on the capital city of Jaxon intent on righting the wrongs done them. Now, one could wonder, "Where was their hope?"

Instead of the swift, even merciful execution ordered by Colonel Rodríguez, these wretched human souls were condemned to a brutal existence of torment and pain.

Hawkins gawked.

The prison complex was a startling change. Instead of the minimal care and attention on the transport, the prison concentrated on maximum control. After passing through a cleansing and decontamination chamber that rubbed their skin raw, the new arrivals were given fresh clothes, some cursory medical attention, and their first decent meal in some months. Nutritional standards were set to optimize the prisoner's work performance. Cleanliness was strictly enforced to reduce disease and a medical infirmary was available. The prison was a smoothly polished metallic complex of interlocking structures where the prisoners were housed in electronically controlled cells with force shields with video monitors. The guards were armed with deadly weapons, as well as electronic whips, stun guns, and sonic whistles that could shock and daze a person.

This is different, but will it be any better?

Zeno was a dwarf planet with a thin, but breathable atmosphere and vast stretches of dry desert lands. The arid land was perennially hot during the day and freezing at night. The little surface water was concentrated in a single modest lake less than twenty kilometers east of the prison complex.

A powerful military fortress—the planet's main defense—lay just north of the prison. A dozen kilometers to the south and separated from the prison by a jagged mountain range, the spaceport boasted a vast array of transport vehicles for loading and unloading cargo ships. The penal colony itself served as a transportation hub from the asteroid mines to the inner planets. The prisoners performed the heavy lifting and operated the equipment for moving millions of tons of material—everything from mine ore heading toward the inner planets, to finished goods returning to the asteroids.

Several days after their arrival, the newcomers were marched into a courtyard like soldiers on parade, lining up with the rest of the prison population. The bright sun beat down on their drab orange shirts and trousers, their faces staring at the array of gray-uniformed guards and officials that surrounded them.

After an hour, or so, of standing in the broiling sun, Jacob Seward, the paunchy balding prison warden, appeared on an overhanging balcony to address these unfortunates.

Seward said, "Welcome! You are now under the authority of the Zeno Penal Colony. You are here because you were weak. You fell into temptation and committed unforgiveable crimes, crimes for which you will be made to pay and pay and pay, because there is no power greater than the law. You must now humble yourselves before its representatives." He paused for effect, then added, "Those who are obedient and obey the rules will find life tolerable, but be forewarned—troublemakers will suffer."

He droned on, extolling his own virtues and belaboring his demands for compliance.

Hawkins looked around and saw fear on the faces of most prisoners. To his surprise, many of the guards wore the same expression.

What are they afraid of?

After an hour of this diatribe, venting the dark suspicions that festered within him, Seward came down from the balcony and stalked around the yard, sizing up the new arrivals. He returned a salute to the chief of the guards and nodded approvingly at the spotless yard and rigid array of guards in their parade uniform.

Seward cast his shifty glance at suspicious-looking individuals in line, darting from one row of prisoners to the next, his prominent hawk nose leading the way. Several times he stopped and spoke to older prisoners as if they were his friends. Hawkins made a mental note marking these as his toadies.

When he caught sight of Hawkins, he leaned forward a little too eagerly, "You there. What's your name?"

"Hawkins."

"I thought so. I've had word of you. Who've you been conspiring with? What treachery are you about?" His thick brows lowered into a wrathful glare and he raised his fist, ready to strike.

Despite the oppressive one-hundred-and-ten-degree temperature, Hawkins remained mute and unflinching.

Not now.

Seward said, "I'll have you know, I can spot conspiracies and squash them flat. Don't think you can hide from me."

Hawkins bit his lip, rather than make a caustic reply. His eyes scanned the older prisoners to look for any signs that the warden's behavior was unusual. The tense atmosphere in the yard seemed to raise the heat a notch.

Annoyed by Hawkins' silence, Seward said, "Your face is a mask of guilt. Remember this; I will beat your bad ways out of you, if I find the slightest disobedience. It would be a pity to have to change your sentence from life, to death, but I will not hesitate to execute mutinous troublemakers."

The warden returned to his place on the balcony and ordered, "Chief, have the prisoners pass in parade."

As they started the procession, a section guard held his hand up to stop one group of prisoners. "Halt. Stand fast. Get the doctor."

"What? What's this? Why have they stopped? Who has countermanded my orders?" cried the warden.

"Sir, a prisoner collapsed. I stopped the men to get him help," said the guard, his voice trembling.

Furious, Seward roared, "Insubordination! Resume the review immediately. Get the sick man out of the way. Chief, I want that guard placed on report. I'll have no insubordination here."

Guards scurried to obey.

"You'll be sorry. You'll be sorry, I promise you!" screamed the warden.

The chief of the guards tried to intervene, "He was only doing his duty, sir."

"Conspiracy! You're in it, together."

The face of the chief blanched. He titled his head down and angled his face away.

Seward ordered the chief of guards to have the troublesome guard whipped.

Maintaining discipline among headstrong prisoners left no room for discussion. Each guard had several electric shock and sonic weapons to control prisoners. A stiff jolt was usually, all they needed. Such spur-of-the-moment punishment was common. However for serious cases, the electronic whip was used to flog problematic prisoners and occasionally, disobedient guards.

The unfortunate guard's pleas for mercy were ignored as he was tied to the whipping post in the middle of the yard. Under the watchful eyes of the guards, any prisoner who flinched, or turned away received a jolt from a stun gun. When the delinquent guard finally collapsed, he was dragged away to the infirmary.

Seward seemed renewed by the event and he left the yard.

The guards remained at attention and the prisoners weren't dismissed immediately. Hawkins looked about curiously. Seward reappeared briefly, taking a quick look around the yard as if trying to catch anyone out of position. Satisfied there was nothing more to see, he said, "Ah, bah!" and disappeared into his headquarters.

At last, the chief of guards ordered, "Officers, dismiss your sections and march the prisoners back to their cells."

Is the warden a paranoid psychotic?

5

A TIMELY INTERVENTION

Prison had unyielding walls, callous guards, and harsh realities—there were no flowers in prison, no acts of kindness or warmth, no smiles of friendship or helping hands. Zeno sapped the will and killed the spirit, leaving each to find his own way to preserve his self-respect.

For the most part, Hawkins survived both the warden's whipping post and the hierarchy of villainy within the walls. Over time, however, Zeno left its mark on Joshua. He had endured the malnourishment of the transport ship and survived sonic shocks from the guards, but the constant bullying of the prison thugs demoralized him. Cringing whenever someone approached, his erstwhile eagerness disappeared, replaced by empty lethargy and lackluster eyes.

Late one afternoon, during the prisoners' hour of exercise in the courtyard, Hawkins found one of Seward's toadies, harassing Joshua. Tall, slender, and agile, with a brutish ugly face, Lasseter maintained his gang authority by victimizing the more vulnerable inmates.

Stepping between them, Hawkins caught Lasseter's hand as the bully was about to strike Joshua.

Lasseter growled, "Stay out of this, it's a personal matter."

"This is personal—to me," said Hawkins.

Lasseter had assessed Joshua as easy prey, but Hawkins had the eyes of a predator.

While three of Lasseter's cronies moved behind him, Hawkins asked, "Aren't you concerned about acting so openly in the courtyard?"

The three men hesitated, but Lasseter laughed, "Ha-ha. The guards know better than to interfere with my sport."

Hawkins had never learned to curb his temper or his tongue. He said, "Given your standing with the warden, that may be true for you, but what about your buddies? Do they have a stake in your misadventure?"

"What nonsense are you spewing? You're buying trouble for yourself," Lasseter threatened.

Instead of showing fear, or respect, as Lasseter had hoped, Hawkins relaxed. He waved Joshua behind him and stood, arms crossed, daring Lasseter to try something.

The hot sun beat down on them and a soft dry breeze barely stirred the sandy ground.

Moving a step closer, Lasseter bared his teeth. "I'll show you," he snarled, but when Hawkins flashed a grin instead of flinching, he hesitated and spewed out a string of foul words into Hawkins's face.

"I fear we are not likely to become friends," said Hawkins with wry grin.

Lasscter's thugs chortled.

Hawkins threw back his shoulders and took a step closer to Lasseter, his footsteps gouging craters in the sandy surface. He addressed the thugs, "You're in your gang to make a profit, right? How much profit do you expect to make here? It wouldn't be in your interest to take part in any disagreement between Lasseter and me."

Lasseter's eyes blackened at the doubt on his men's faces. He said, "I need no help dealing with the likes of you," and pulled a wicked-looking eight inch blade from behind his back. Furious at the insolence, he leaped forward and stabbed at Hawkins in one quick motion.

With a sharp intake of breath, Hawkins reacted instinctively to block the knife and grab Lasseter's hand. He twisted it down and away, forcing him to drop the weapon.

Gasping in pain, Lasseter cursed and yelped, "Get this human trash, or you'll all pay later."

As the three men approached, Hawkins looked warily from side to side to assess his chances.

I don't think these men have had combat training.

Hawkins sidestepped the first man, tripping him as he lunged past. He hit the second man full on the chin with the butt of his palm and pushed him, staggering in the loose footing, to one side. Ducking under the swinging fist of the third man, he came up fast and punched him in the stomach.

"Ooff!"

The man doubled over, gasping for breath.

Hawkins put his hands on his hips and said, "Ha! Gentlemen, I beg you to reconsider. If you persist, this lesson will proceed to a more advanced level."

Again the ruffians hesitated, unsure of what they saw behind Hawkins's eyes: it was something unequivocal that frightened them.

Hawkins saw rage burning in Lasseter's eyes and thought . . .

Rage is a destructive emotion. It rips and stabs and tears with blind hate—it kills reason and spawns misjudgment.

Hawkins rocked forward, balancing on the balls of his feet, waiting for Lasseter's blunder.

Lasseter kicked out blindly and Hawkins felt the blow on his shin. Cupping his hands, Hawkins slapped his attacker's ears, and Lasseter staggered back with a howl, blood trickling down his neck.

Back on offense, the henchmen circled, looking for an advantage. From a boot sheath, one pulled out a large serrated knife, a knife for fighting, for killing. This wasn't a simple brawl any longer—now it was life and death.

By now the other prisoners in the courtyard had formed a large circle around the combatants, shouting and yelling. But despite Lasseter's unpopularity, no one stepped forward to aid Hawkins. Likewise, the guards stayed outside the 10-foot chain-link fence with razor wire tops; content to watch the fracas from a safe distance.

As if on cue, the trio rushed toward him, and Hawkins sucked in a quick breath. He leaned sharply to the right and abruptly swept his left foot in a high arc. His heel hit the closest man's hand, sending the knife sailing across the sand and the man reeling backward. Continuing his pivot, Hawkins drove his shoulder into the second man's chest. Before the last thug could react to the sudden onslaught, Hawkins grabbed him, hurled him to the ground, and kicked him in the stomach.

Behind him, Lasseter recovered his knife and came at Hawkins, the knife raised to strike.

"Look out!" shouted Joshua, "behind you!"

Lasseter's knife thrust might have penetrated Hawkins's lung, or perhaps his heart, if not for Joshua. Dashing forward without thinking, his shove deflected Lasseter's arm just enough so that the blade ripped through the coarse fabric of Hawkins's jumpsuit and slithered down his ribs, slicing off a hunk of flesh.

"Much obliged, my young friend," said Hawkins, wiping blood from his back.

Sweat rolling down his body, Lasseter gave a roar and swung his knee at his opponent's groin, but Hawkins parried the blow and sent him sprawling.

One of Lasseter's henchmen was back on his feet and charged Hawkins like a raging bull.

"Aaaahhhh," he yelled, wrapping his arms around Hawkins and knocking him to the ground. All four men swarmed him, punching, and kicking.

"Stop, stop," Joshua screamed, launching his gangly body into the mass of pounding arms and legs. They knocked him aside, but the momentary lapse gave Hawkins a chance to grab hold of a flailing arm and pull himself up.

Breathing hard, Hawkins gave free reign to his combat training.

WHACK!

A vicious karate chop.

It nearly broke the arm that was headed for his throat.

CRACK!

He landed a solid kick right on an exposed knee, and the man howled clutching at his leg as the splintered knee-cap collapsed.

The third man managed to land a punch on Hawkins's jaw, leaving an imprint of coarse knuckles on his cheek and snapping his head back. As the thug pulled his arm back for another swing, Hawkins recovered and struck first. The flat of his hand chopped the man's exposed throat.

"Aarrgh!" the man croaked, eyes bulging.

Parrying the jab of Lasseter's knife, Hawkins grabbed the gang leader's collar, snapping the man's head down to meet the upward thrust of Hawkins' knee. Lasseter crumpled to the sand, out cold.

With their leader out of the fray, the three henchmen had no desire to continue. They stayed down, panting and grimacing in pain, unable to do more than glare their hate.

Taking a deep breath, Hawkins spat out a mouthful of blood and started to walk away. Just then, Seward entered the courtyard with several guards trailing as usual.

The ring of prisoners scattered.

"A subversive assembly," cried Seward, raw with anger and disappointed to see his toady on the ground.

"No…" Hawkins started, but the guards grabbed him, yanking his arms behind his back, and threatening him with their stun guns.

"You lie to my face?" screamed Seward, his imagined accusation fixing itself as truth in his mind. "Who conspired with you? Hey? Nothing to say? Well, I know ways of loosening obstinate tongues."

Hawkins was chained to a post.

WHIZZZZ!

The electronic whip shot out again and again cutting deep into his flesh. The pain was so severe that he imagined the surrounding prison walls closing around him, intent on crushing the life out of him. He wanted to scream at the lunacy, but soon lost consciousness.

6

A FRIEND

Several days later, the med-tech cracked, "I've not seen many bodies as scarred as yours. You should take better care of yourself."

"Sound advice," said Hawkins, curling his lips into a grin.

The med-tech tended him with the meager facilities available. He asked, "How bad is the pain?"

Hawkins said, "I've known worse." He had a stale sour taste in his mouth from medication and his back burned from the electric lash burns. His limbs ached from the healing wounds and bruises. He found turning his neck was still stiff and painful, and while his eyes burned, he was able to see clearly, despite his throbbing headache.

The medic said, "You need twenty-four hours in a regeneration chamber, but we don't have one. I'm sorry, but I've done all I can for you."

"Don't worry about me," said Hawkins cynically, "I always land on my feet—eventually."

The Zeno spaceport was capable of launching and landing a variety of spacecraft. Located a dozen kilometers from the major population center, in order to mitigate risk from a catastrophic failure, it was surrounded by a large safety range with tracking stations. When cargo ship, too large to land, arrived, they parked it in orbit and used space tugs to transfer cargo.

When Hawkins returned to work, as part of a loading crew that used robots and physical exoskeleton enhancements, he helped move cargo. While working in the loading docks, the prisoners enjoyed a greater freedom than in their highly controlled electronic force field cells, though they were closely watched by guards.

During the noon break, he disengaged from the exoskeleton and sat on the ground eating a nutrient bar and sipping water from a flask.

He looked up as a stranger approached—tall, with fair skin and hair, and intelligent blue eyes, wearing a friendly smile.

"Aaron Hale," he said, extending his hand. "You saved my life at Newport Hospital—for that, I'm obliged."

Hale was the older of the two men. Their similarities and differences were reflected on their faces. While both exhibited tremendous vitality and drive, Hawkins' revealed his aggressive, impulsive, iron-will. Hale's calm, self-disciplined, and adaptable demeanor, spoke for itself.

As Hawkins shook the offered hand, he said, "I hold no one under obligation for my actions, for I put no trust in gratitude. I put my faith in myself and act as my conscience dictates."

"Are you not in prison because the law declared that 'he who aids a rebel is a rebel'?"

"I didn't say I've always profited from my conscience."

"Do you consider yourself a rebel now?"

Hawkins shook his head and asked, "How did you come to be a rebel?"

"I taught history at the University. When the government's injustices reached into the classroom and started to claim my students, I had to resist. Now I'm the rebel leader within this prison."

Hawkins munched on his nutrient bar and said nothing.

Hale said, "I watched your brawl with Lasseter, the other day."

"Yet, you felt no obligation to lend a hand?" Hawkins asked with a wry smile.

"It never occurred to me that you needed one," said Hale, matching his smile. "But be on your guard. You have many enemies."

His eyes flashing, Hawkins retorted, "Perhaps you judge me too lightly."

Hale sized Hawkins up. After a long minute, he said, "Last year you were a Marine, fighting Hellion soldiers. A few months ago you tangled with Colonel Rodríguez and Jaxon soldiers. Last week, you clashed with Lasseter and his gang, and got whipped for your trouble. You seem to have a visceral fondness for acquiring enemies."

"As you say," said Hawkins, lifting his chin. "I do not lack antagonists."

Hale chuckled, "True enough, but whatever your reasons, you haven't become a rebel."

Hawkins instinctively liked Hale, but remained silent, cautious, and uncommitted.

Hale said, "I would have thought that the persecution you've endured would have convinced you of the justice of our cause. Why don't you join me, along with the decent men who believe in a better way of life and are willing to fight for it?"

"My primary interest is getting off Zeno," said Hawkins, considering whether he could trust his instincts.

Hale tried a different tach, "The war against Hellion has been going poorly for years. The laws in peacetime are very different than the rules of war, and in recent years, President Victor has successfully eroded our constitutional rights and stolen a fortune for himself in the process. Our government is no longer a democracy. Abuse and torture are wide spread, and not just against our enemy. You yourself are an example of the rampant injustice. Victor has offered our people nothing but vacuous schemes to defeat Hellion, while we slide into a corrupt dictatorship that spouts Orwellian slogans."

Hawkins said, "You speak of the longings of the people, but Victor claims the rebels are backed by Hellion and he limits civil liberties in the name of security."

"You take the measure of man not by the best acts he performs, but by the worst acts he is capable of. If he can slaughter innocents, then it doesn't matter how much he has thrown in the charity baskets. Victor is a bad man. He has enriched his family with phony contracts to divert money into their pockets. He's never met a conspiracy theory he hasn't subscribed to. How do you think a man like Seward got to be in charge of Zeno?"

Hawkins said, gruffly, "It was the people who elected that greedy politician and stood by while he subverted the republic."

"True, we bear the fault of complacency for waiting far too long. But now we are angry enough to take action and restore our democracy."

"It may be too late."

"You didn't think so when you came to protect those in the hospital, or when you confronted Colonel Rodríguez to stop a massacre."

"And look where that has gotten me, facing off against a prison gang and a paranoid warden."

"So now that you've experienced it firsthand, perhaps you've a better idea of the injustice of this government."

"Yes, prison does tend to focus the mind. I'm convinced that Victor must go, but it must happen without opening the door for a Hellion invasion."

"An interesting prospect," said Hale.

"In the meantime, escape is the best plan," said Hawkins.

"Are you making headway with an escape plan?"

"I've gotten absolutely nowhere."

"You don't have to face that challenge alone."

"No?"

"The rebels in this prison have band together. A man of your skills and talents would be useful."

Hawkins said, "Since Fate has thrown us to together once more, I feel compelled to take advantage of the opportunity."

"You're pretty good with equipment," Hale observed. "I can help get you assigned to a job in machine maintenance. It's easier than manual labor, or running heavy equipment, and comes with extra privileges."

"Including access to sensitive areas?"

"Don't get ahead of yourself. It'll take a lot to escape this place."

"I'm prepared to make it happen, but I could use help."

"If we did succeed," said Hale reflectively, "I know a rebel base in the asteroids that would support us. It's called Echo."

Hawkins could detect no chicanery in Hale's words, only earnest sentiment. He said, "We're a lot alike; you and I. Our personalities are stamped with resilient beliefs and a powerful will to succeed."

"Does that portent cooperation, or competition?'

Still reluctant to commit himself wholeheartedly, Hawkins said, "We'll see."

"You don't know your own story."

"What story? That I restored the hospital shield?"

"No, anyone could have done that. The story of a Marine who stood up to a hundred Jaxon soldiers and single-handedly stopped a massacre."

"No one would believe that," said Hawkins, shaking his head. Though his denial might have been mistaken for modesty, Hawkins harbored a brutal honesty that held him accountable for all his shortcomings and failures and prevented him from taking satisfaction in praises.

"You're already a folk hero with the people. Of course, the government hates your story. That's why you wound up here."

Hawkins considered that for a moment, then his mind wandered and he thought of the attractive doctor who had made such an impression on him. He asked, "Do you know what happened to the people from the hospital?"

"The men are here. The women and children are in detention camps."

"What about the hospital personnel?"

"They remain under surveillance and are forced to work in government medical centers."

"Everyone?"

"Was there someone in particular you were interested in?" asked Hale.

Yes, I'm interested.

Hawkins said, "Dr. Palmer."

"Alyssa?" responded Hale, his voice rising in surprise. Hawkins saw a crack in his composure and calm demeanor.

Just as surprised, Hawkins frowned and said, "Yes. Alyssa."

Jealous?

7

HATCHING A PLAN

A maintenance tunnel ran underground from the Zeno spaceport, passed under the fortress, and ended under the prison complex. It had security hatches every kilometer, but during the workday while they moved cargo, or made repairs on heavy equipment, there were short periods when prisoners were able to meet secretly in the dark dank interlacing enclosure. There they avoided the scrutiny of guards and video monitors while exchanging tidbits of news that would filter into the prison gossip mill. War stories and tales of merciless government repression were interspersed with scurrilous stories of violence by rebels. Each rumor circulated around the prison walls with equal velocity stoking the inmates' appetite to escape from the endless grind of hard physical labor and cruel oppressive captivity.

On one occasion, Hawkins found a few moments to get together with Hale, out of sight of prying eyes.

Hale said, "The chance of escaping this hellhole with all its manifold security controls is so slim that you have to reach true desperation before attempting it."

"The only prison you can't break out of is the one you build for yourself—in here," said Hawkins tapping his head.

Hale said, "There are electronic sensors on the prison cells, around the guard tower, and throughout the barbed wire fences. Add video surveillance and numerous guards, none of which are easily thwarted, and we will still need a way to escape from the planet."

"There are numerous small cargo freighters in port on any given day. We have access to them while we're loading and unloading them. It might be possible to steal a small ship and depart this rat hole before Seward kills us all."

"Escape would require a diverse and talented crew. I know a few rebels who might be willing to take a chance on escape, but none of them can operate nuclear reactors, or astrogate," said Hale.

Hawkins stood up and swung his arms wide. "Look around—this place has men of every known skill and talent. As long as we're discreet, we can recruit the men we need. All we have to do is offer them the opportunity."

"But even if we were able to steal a ship, it would be shot down by the heavy guns from the fortress, as soon as it was detected."

"We'll need a talented computer programmer to hack the security systems."

"What about your young friend, Joshua?"

Hawkins agreed, "Yes. He can be trusted and he has a natural talented for coding software. If we can get him access to a cybersecurity terminal, he might be the one to disable key sensor components."

"I have an idea about how to do that and I know the coordinates of rebel base Echo in the asteroid belt that would give us sanctuary, if we ever made it that far."

Great!

"We have assets, some of which are hidden, some of which will take persuasion, but how we use them, will decide if we survive. It only remains for us to be creative."

"Time may reveal our solution."

Hawkins said, "If I can talk to some of the men and explain my plan, I may win their trust."

Hale said, "You already have a cache of goodwill among those who heard of your stand at the Newport hospital and witnessed your fight with Lasseter's gang."

Hale continued, "To recruit specialized techs, we can only approach candidates we trust not to betray us, who can keep their mouths shut. They might turn us in, or want to join even if they are not invited, or they might talk too much to others and start dangerous rumors."

"Caution is essential. Don't worry, I'll find the men we need—including an astrogator and nuclear engineer."

Hawkins chuckled, "We'll put together a crew that can handle anything space can throw at them."

A few days later, true to his word, Hale succeeded in gathering a dozen men in the maintenance tunnel by bribing a guard to look the other way.

Hawkins shook each man's hand as Hale introduced them. They remained standing in a circle while he said, "I've wanted to meet you and offer you a chance—a chance to escape this unhappy planet. I'll admit, it's not much of a chance, but if it's only one chance in a million of finding a life away from Seward and his whip, it's one I'm willing to take."

The darkness hid the uncertainty that he knew was on their faces.

Hope. I must give them hope.

"Some of you have heard about what happened at the Newport hospital. Many of you saw me brawl with Lasseter's gang," said Hawkins, "I'm willing to stand up and fight for you as well."

A short squat man said, "OK, Hawkins, make your pitch and make it quick, before the guards get curious."

Hawkins said, "It may be possible for us to steal a cargo ship that will take us far away from this hell-hole. There's a rebel base in the asteroids where we can find shelter and support—a life of freedom and decency. I believe, together, we can get there."

Shaking his head, the squat man said, "I've only five more years to serve. If I attempt to escape there's no going back."

Hale asked, "Will Seward even let you live five more years?"

There was a universal groan.

One man spoke out, "Fine talk, but I can't even dodge my cell surveillance."

"We have someone who can disable certain prison sensors and deceive some of the planetary radars," said Hale.

A huge grizzly bear of a man said, "My name is Bill Simmons, everyone calls me Gunny, and I'm willing to take a gamble with you. Can you use a weapons tech?"

Hawkins curled his lip into a fulsome smile and laughed, "Ha!" He extended his hand and Gunny's giant paw closed around it. He gasped, "Easy, big fellow, I'm going to need that back."

Several men laughed.

"I want you to know, that I'm going," said Gunny, his voice filled with emotion. "I'm going to leave this place and never look back."

"Go? Go where?" asked the squat man.

"Away! Anywhere! Just anywhere away from this accursed planet," said Gunny.

"Alone?" said the squat man his sullen frown growing across his broad face.

"Alone, or not, I'm going."

Gunny had full-of-fun red cheeks and a surprisingly jolly disposition despite his intimidating size. He was the kind of man Hawkins wanted.

I like this big fellow.

Next a man of ordinary features, with a quiet manner, and a ragged appearance, spoke up, "My name is

Robert Mitchel and what I want to know is can you use an engineer?"

Hawkins raised his eyebrow and said, "Definitely." He sensed he was winning them over. He looked around the circle, from face to face, and asked, "Are you with me?"

A chorus of *yes, yes, yes,* erupted—including the squat man, who turned out to be an astrogator named Williams.

Hawkins told Joshua, "Your job will be to disable the prison cell sensors and the planetary radars when we're ready to make our break."

Joshua said, "If you can get me access to the controls of the AI sensor systems, I can manipulate them so the guards will think we're in our cell. I can also hack the planet's long range sensors to prevent our ship from being detected."

"Are you sure you can do that?" asked Hawkins.

Feeling rejuvenated by his involvement with the escape committee, Joshua said, "You pick the time. I'll deliver."

Hawkins was pleased with this core group. The chief risk was that someone might talk out of turn. Over the next few weeks, he began recruiting former soldiers and crewmen, but then things slowed down. They waited for the right opportunity and it took longer than they anticipated until finally, Hawkins announced, "We're ready."

Hale said, "Then it only remains to find a ship that will serve."

A few days later, they were ready to make their plan a reality.

While assigned to a work detail near the spaceport, Hawkins brought Joshua with him to repair a sensor control terminal. From the control panel, Joshua was able to modify the base's sensors and manipulated the data to disguise radar blips to register as large a meteor instead of a ship. It was merely a matter of size and clarity. The sensors were now giving distorted reports to the sensor tech on duty. The deception would give the rebels a chance to escape in a stolen ship.

"Tomorrow," said Hawkins.

Hale nodded and the word was passed to each of the conspirators.

Everything was ready, but the waiting rubbed the prisoner's nerves raw.

Tomorrow seemed a lifetime away.

8

TWIST OF FATE

The following day—the day of days—there was a twist of Fate.

An unexpected sandstorm shrieked across the Zeno desert with a ferocity that dwarfed past humbler cyclones. The wind and sand ate away the veneer of buildings, ships, and vehicles alike, stripping their superficial irregularities, and leaving behind smooth surfaces streaked with stains. The streets were clogged with sand and strewn with branches and debris. Heavy machinery left outside was choked with grit. Outside the prison, the colony's inhabitants huddled in their fragile prefabricated shelters, waiting for the onslaught to end. The storm obscured all evidence of human activity and the colony looked like a dusty gray ruin.

"Stopped, before we even got started," said Hale, crestfallen.

Hawkins knew he was right to be concerned, but wrong to think there wasn't a remedy.

Hawkins shook his head. "Not stopped; only delayed. We'll push our plans out by twenty-four hours. How much difference can one day make? Besides, the whole complex will be in chaos after this storm. It'll make stealing a ship that much easier."

Hale said, "OK. We'll leave the modified sensors in place and go forward with our plan at 0600."

But the next morning, while Warden Jacob Seward was busy torturing a prisoner at the whipping post, a tremendous roar shook the entire colony. The blast drowned out the prisoner's agonized wails and reverberated in the thin atmosphere. All eyes turned skyward.

Incredulous, Seward screamed, "Attack! We're under attack! Hellion is attacking." It was a tragic flaw in his temperament to always arrive at the essential point, too late. He shook his fists skyward in wild fury and ran for shelter.

Guards and prisoners alike scattered like sheep. A weapons battery just outside the prison opened fire, sending a missile into the sky.

Safely inside the prison bastion, Seward turned furiously on his guards. "What happened at the fortress? They must have all been asleep to let this enemy sneak up on us."

With each crash of falling missiles, Seward screamed orders that defied logic, sending his forces scurrying aimlessly in disarray.

Seward foolishly ordered his men to gather in a vulnerable location that was immediately hit by an accurately aimed missile. Thus the enemy was able to dispatch a significant amount of Seward's ground forces while simultaneously rendering the facility, ineffective as a prison—the prisoners were set.

After establishing contact with the fortress, they confirmed that a Hellion warship was orbiting the planet firing weapons down onto the battlements. The warship's fire was focused primarily on the fortress and as it reduced the defenses, the ship moved into a lower orbit to improve the effectiveness of its weapons.

The warship was a frigate, a single raider: not a major combatant, but formidable nonetheless. It was equipped with ray guns for ship-to-ship combat and missiles for planetary bombardment. The ship had used stolen transponder codes from a Jaxon ship to get close, but that hoax wasn't even necessary. Joshua's computer virus had utterly fooled the long-range sensor techs.

All of Hawkins' crafty plans to confuse the long range sensors to further his escape, had made it easier for this interloper to take advantage and seize the prize out from under him. The warship had succeeded so well that it aroused no suspicion until it was within optimal firing range. Then it was too late for the fortress to raise its shields to mount a proper defense, consequently, it was significantly reduced after only a few minutes of bombardment. He assumed the Hellion would destroy the fortress and then land troops to sack the spaceport and steal its great wealth.

Hawkins couldn't bear to watch. He stood in the prison courtyard, bitter and frustrated, staring skyward with unseeing eyes. All his careful preparations for escape crumbled around him.

As missiles continued to demolish the prison walls, the prisoners scattered into the surrounding hillside, all except Hawkins and his cadre of conspirators.

But their gloomy faces spoke volumes.

"What infernal bad luck! The Hellion chose to attack on the very day we were set to escape. We will never escape in a ship now. We'd be blown apart," squawked Hale. "If only that sandstorm hadn't delayed us yesterday—of all the infernal bad luck!"

His face set, Hawkins stood tight-lipped with hand to his brow to shade his eyes as he looked up.

Clenching his fist and raising it skyward, he said, "Attacking the colony appears to dash our plans of escape."

Suddenly, he threw back his head and laughed, "Ha! Bad luck?! This may prove to be, just as much, a blessing, as a curse?"

"What do you mean?" Hale asked, bewildered.

Hawkins said, "We need only adjust our plans, slightly, to insert ourselves into the equation of this battle and make it play out in our favor."

Debating the odds, he watched the trails of smoke as the missiles plunged to earth and saw the vessel—a tiny streak—maneuver and fire again. Would the missiles kill them all before they could escape?

"How is that possible?" asked Hale.

"Instead of stealing a small cargo vessel, we will steal something bigger and better."

"Bigger?"

"Yes!"

"And better?"

"Yes," said Hawkins. "Where you see disaster, I see opportunity. Where you feel despair, I feel hope. Listen to me, do what I tell you…and before this day is out, you will taste victory!"

At Hawkins's words, his men's gloom vanished. They turned eager faces to him, desperate to believe they still had a chance.

"First, find me a dead officer," said Hawkins.

Among the numerous bodies of fallen soldiers, they soon found a captain. Hawkins quickly changed clothes with the officer and took his security key card and told his followers to swap their prison garb for Jaxon uniforms as well. Next Hawkins led them to the armory, using the captain's key card to gain access and distribute weapons.

Finally, he ordered them to the relative safety of the maintenance tunnel.

"Stay there and wait for my signal," he said, "I'll call after the enemy has landed assault troops. Trust me."

Wearing the dead captain's uniform, Hawkins left the prison in a single seat flyer and flew to the fortress. There he found the Jaxon troops in chaos. The dust and debris of broken ramparts and bulkheads were everywhere. The fortress was in a state of devastation and confusion. Its shield strength fluctuated, providing limited protection. Half the heavy weapon systems were already blown up and in a rubble heap. Many of the remaining weapons were not manned, or disabled. None were being properly directed. Many of the garrison men were either dead, or had fled. The remaining soldiers was utterly disheartened and reduced to helplessness by a complete failure of leadership. Only a resolute, but green, lieutenant remained in the fire control center and, he appeared befuddled and completely overwhelmed.

Hawkins went into the control center and faced the lieutenant just as another barrage struck the weak outer shield. The building shook, but the shield held for the moment.

How much longer?

He demanded, "Will you stay here cowering until there is nothing left but ruins?"

Startled the lieutenant replied doggedly, "I will remain at my post until death."

Hawkins saw his own reflection in the young man's eyes. He smiled and said good-naturedly, "Fool, think ahead. If you stay here with the heavy mobile guns, we'll have nothing left to repel a land assault."

The lieutenant appeared stunned.

"Take half these men and the remaining mobile heavy weapons and missile launchers into the surrounding mountains. Set up an ambush along the main road from the port to the city," Hawkins commanded briskly. "I will stay here and defend the fortress as long as possible."

As the lieutenant hesitated, Hawkins goosed him into action. "Look sharp, man! Put that resolve of yours into a worthwhile effort instead of wasting your life here."

Lieutenant was not imaginative, but he was disciplined and recognized a sound plan when he heard it. He realized that Hawkins' orders made more sense than the nonsense orders Seward had spouted, but he asked, "What can you do from here against the enemy?"

"It is always best to let your opponent see what's in your left hand while you pick his pocket with your right. My simple distraction here will move the enemy into position, so you can catch him in the flank when the assault troops land," said Hawkins, feeling exhilarated.

The lieutenant said, "I may lack experience, sir, but I admire the shrewdness of your plan. I'll carry out your orders with all my strength."

"Excellent."

"But sir, shouldn't you let me remain under fire in the fortress while you arrange the ambush?"

"On the contrary, Lieutenant. After giving you time to move the mobile weapons into the mountains, I will abandon the fort—it will probably be rubble by then anyway—then I will lead an assault on the enemy warship with our shuttles."

The lieutenant gasped.

Hawkins said, "Our position demands dreadful sacrifice. In effect, we must consider ourselves—expendable."

"Once again, sir, you assume all the risk. Shouldn't I...."

Hawkins was already thinking ahead. "No, Lieutenant, it will take some finesse to get the shuttles close enough to the warship to do any good. Trust me; you're better used, hidden in the woods with the artillery to ambush the Hellion landing force. If you accomplish that, I'm prepared to lead a surprise attack on the enemy ship."

"Brilliant, sir. I'm sure it'll work."

"Thanks. I hope so. We will be vulnerable in the shuttles. So I would appreciate your restraint in not firing on any shuttle craft until I signal that your help is needed."

"Yes sir, of course, sir," said the lieutenant, his words tumbling over themselves in his eagerness "Just...one more thing, sir, if I may?"

"Yes."

"What...what is the Captain's name? I don't recognize you, I'm sorry to say."

"Captain Hawkins," he replied, suppressing a smirk at the irony. "As it happens, I am newly commissioned in the Jaxon army, and whether that turns out to be a fortunate occurrence for you, or a poorly timed misfortune for me, remains to be seen."

He gave the younger man a friendly shove. "Now off with you."

The lieutenant rushed to fulfill his orders.

Hawkins took over the defense of the crumbling fortress. He issued a string of rapid orders to those around him, starting with enhancing the power to the Unified Quantum Field (UQF) force shields. Next, he identified groups of weapons that would fire in unison from a selected battery commander.

Hawkins ordered, "Fire."

Luck favored him and his first barrage damaged the warship as she maneuvered over the planet. The men were cheered.

The lieutenant gave a final salute and his small caravan of men and weapons set off. Soon he was hiding along the road in ambush, waiting.

Hawkins remained in the fort's control center which was still the main target of the enemy. He changed the firing sequence. He went from weapon station, to weapon station, setting the parameters of each to ensure the most effective fire. His vigor stimulated the skeleton crew and the fort's fire became more effective. He had weapons stop firing when the ship targeted near them. This let the enemy think those weapons had been destroyed. Later he returned them to service, catching the ship off guard, while it was entering a lower orbit to prepare for a landing. This offered Hawkins an opportunity to score some effective hits. His effort was enough to cause the warship to return to a higher orbit.

The men responded to this temporary reprieve with a cheer and looked to Hawkins as if he were a miracle worker. However, the warship returned to a stable firing position and began battering the fort once more.

Daring, as always, Hawkins continued to bait and switch his fire for as long as his weapons remained, but after an hour of cat and mouse the game was up, and a series of targeted bursts from the warship found their mark. In a burst of light and noise, his remaining heavy weapons were reduced to red-hot slag.

Once again the warship entered lower orbit and readied to land its assault force. The warship fired a final devastating barrage which struck an ammunition dump. It caused a horrific explosion that tore the fort apart and shook the ground stronger than any earthquake had ever done. It tossed Hawkins high into the air and whacked him hard onto the ground . . .

. . . in that instant, he was four years old again; listening to his mother say that his father would not be coming home. Then, he was outside, running as fast as his underdeveloped legs could carry him, seeking to escape an unfair world, until exhausted, he finally collapsed and lay on the ground looking up at the heavens . . .

When Hawkins opened his eyes, he lay on the ground looking up at the sky through the outstretched branches of a burnt out tree. It was several seconds before he was able to struggle painfully to his feet. His skull felt as if it were split in two and warm blood trickled freely down his left ear and cheek. Nevertheless, he dismissed the pain, as well as his visions of the past—because there were things he needed to do—in the here and now.

He ordered the remaining soldiers to abandon the fort and seek shelter.

He said, "Your work is done. I still have more to do. Now go."

Several hesitated, wanting to remain with him, but he stared them down and ordered them to join the lieutenant.

With the fort overwhelmed, Hawkins made his way toward the maintenance tunnel near the spaceport. It was now time to put the second half of his plan into action—and launch a surprise attack on the warship.

9

HIJACK

The smoke and damage from the bombardment hid Hawkins as he crawled into the pitch black subterranean maintenance tunnel. He had to feel the walls and guess where his fellow conspirators were. A rat squealed and scamper past.

"Hawkins!" called Hale, his voice high pitched and tense.

"Yes. Is everyone else here?"

"We've been waiting for you."

"Gather around," Hawkins said. "Things have not played out as we originally imagined, but we'll succeed, if we act without hesitation."

"Just tell us what to do, Jamie," said Gunny, eager as always.

"Yeah, we're ready," said Mitchel.

"Are the lookouts set?" asked Hawkins.

"Everywhere they're needed."

BANG!

The men all jumped at the sudden noise, right next to them.

"Sorry, sorry, it's only me," said Gunny. "I think I knocked over a tool chest."

Everyone breathed a sigh of relief.

"Follow me," said Hawkins.

They scurried, much like the rats around them, feeling their way through the wet stink of the passages to where the outlet emerged behind the shuttle bay.

A half dozen Hellion guards were patrolling around the shuttlecraft, relaxed and confident, believing the attack was going well. They failed to notice Hawkins and his men sneaking ever closer, until it was too late. The skirmish was brief, violent, and over in a minute with many of the Hellion unconscious, or dead.

Securing the shuttles, Hawkins now switched into a Hellion officer's uniform. His men switched from their Jaxon uniforms into uniforms of the fallen Hellion guards. In a few minutes, they were aboard the shuttles along with their Hellion prisoners.

As the shuttles took off, they overheard the Hellion landing force reporting that they had been waylaid and taken casualties. Just as Hawkins had predicted, the ground troops had marched from the spaceport over the mountain road and straight into the lieutenant's ambush, suffering devastating losses.

Hawkins signaled the warship, *Destiny*, "This is Captain Hawkins of the assault force, we have casualties aboard. Have medical staff standing by."

The officer acknowledged, "Medical staff will be waiting at the docking bay."

The shuttles carried over a hundred of Hawkins' men and though he estimated that there were over two hundred defenders remaining on the ship, he counted on the element of surprise and the fact that most of the ship's crew would be at their stations unarmed.

The deck shuddered as the shuttle settled into the docking bay. A green light flashed when the pressure was equalized and they were able to disembark.

"Permission to come aboard?" asked Hawkins in a professional manner, saluting as he did so.

The gangplank watch stander didn't recognize Hawkins, but responded to his rank and saluted back. He said, "Permission granted, sir."

As the medical staff began unloading the unconscious Hellion guards, Hawkins and his men, quickly subdued them.

Then Hawkins said, "Mitchel, take your men and secure engineering."

"Will do, Captain."

"Gunny, you and your men hit the armory and communications. Hale, you and the rest follow me to the bridge." Without waiting to seeing if anyone followed him, Hawkins ran off at full speed.

He briskly stepped through the security hatch and into the operations compartment and passed silent machinery that had sustained battle damage. Few pieces of equipment were operating and a few others were being serviced by crewmen.

When he entered in the corridor leading to the bridge, Hawkins crouched and peeked around the corner. He darted from one position to another. There were a number of Hellion crewmen working and laughing in a relaxed good-natured way, thinking they had already won the battle.

Hawkins jumped up and startled them.

"Gentlemen, surrender peacefully and you will not be harmed," he offered.

For a long moment, the bridge watch gaped at him, trying to identify the man in the officer's uniform who stood so boldly before them.

"Who are you?" one finally asked.

"I am Captain Hawkins, and you are now my prisoners," he said, pointing his pistol at each of them in turn.

"What? Why?" came the perplexed response.

"These men and I are escaped prisoners from the planet below. We have taken over your ship."

For a long moment, they only stared at him. Then, the Hellion crew who were armed drew their weapons and opened fire.

Hawkins and his men fell back into the corridor and laid down heavy fire, forcing the Hellion crew to the far end of the bridge. With Hawkins providing cover, Joshua made his way to the ship's AI control panel and quickly gained control of the communications system."

While Hawkins and several of his men laid down covering fire, Joshua was able to tap into the ship's AI control pane and gained control of the communication system.

Joshua reported, "It looks like there is fighting in engineering and elsewhere on the ship. Lights and power are out in most of the ship."

The Hellion crew resisted throughout the ship, however, without their communications systems they weren't able to mount a coherent defense. They continued to fight resolutely in small bands, wherever they could. They fired pistols, rifles, and tossed a few grenades.

One blast stunned Hawkins.

Why has everything gotten so quiet?

His senses told him something was seriously wrong; at first he couldn't hear and when his hearing returned the sounds were the wrong noises; the rumbling of machines and the humming of equipment were absent. Instead, loud cries of anguish and the jostling of crewmen combating fires reached his ears. It took several minutes before he shook off the effects of the concussion. He took a deep breath. The acrid fumes of fire stung his nose.

One Hellion crewman charged. A shot rang out; he staggered and fell down, mortally wounded.

Hawkins's men kept up a steady fire, and under his direction, they drove the enemy back. Some of the Hellion men were struggling to get into battle armor and gather their weapons even as Hawkins fired at them.

A blast burned through the hatch, he was hiding behind.

"Ugh—" he cried from the scorching heat of the near miss. The plasma blast splattered off the bulkhead next to Hawkins.

This was followed by a series of earsplitting explosions. KABOOOM! KABOOOM!

The shocking roar briefly rendered Hawkins nearly deaf. He instinctively raised his hands to his ears.

What happened?

Footsteps approached. It was Hale bringing up more men to the bridge. As he turned around, he found Hale at his side, his face eager and ready to go forward. Calmer now, Hawkins observe several Hellion men swarming into the compartment.

Focus!

As Hawkins climbed up behind them, Hale opened fire and engaged them in the firefight. Together they methodically targeted the Hellion crew.

Rapid firing his projectile gun, Hawkins soon heard the click of empty chambers. Letting the gun fall from his hands, he pulled out a grenade and hurled it forward.

Got to keep fighting . . .

After a few moments of agreeable respite, he was beginning to get a glimmer of optimism when . . .

Peering over his shoulder into the dark, he tripped on some debris. As he crashed to the deck, he lay still and listened.

Thoughts flashed past him.

Where are they?

As Hawkins twisted around a corner, he crashed into a panel that knocked him back and spun him around. His legs were exhausted and unwilling to move. Leaning against the bulkhead, like a dead weight, he slid slowly down to the deck and rested for a minute.

He held his breath.

Who is that?

In the dim light, vague phantoms lurked nearby.

"Jamie?"

It was Hale! From behind the bridge, he had picked off several of the more exposed crewmen.

Hawkins continued to move toward the fiercest fighting. Twice he felt the heat of near miss plasma blasts. Then the wave of the action washed past him and he found several men moaning nearby on the deck. The wounded men sought shelter behind a panel. As the fighting madness ebbed away, Hawkins realized the nearby crewmen would die soon without medical assistance.

Hawkins grabbed a discarded rifle and launched forward. A few men rallied toward him, and together they charged one more time, but the group was insufficient to drive the Hellion off the bridge.

Each frenzied violent assault was met by courageous resistance in a final desperate act of passion. Finally, Hawkins found himself, fighting hand to hand with *Destiny's* remaining senior officer. The struggle ended when Hawkins conked him on the head and rendered him senseless.

The final Hellion resistance collapsed.

The internal contest was over.

Despite having claimed the ship, they had no time to rest. Somehow they had to defend the ship and move her out of range of the planet's weapons.

Hawkins acted swiftly. Before long Mitchel had the engines operating and they were able to move the ship.

Amid the smoke and debris on the planet's surface, Seward stormed about in a seething lather. He ordered, "Lieutenant, fire your mobile weapons batteries at that ship."

"But sir, our troops are fighting on that ship under Captain Hawkins," replied the confused Lieutenant.

"You fool. You utter imbecile!" Seward raged throwing his hands in the air. "Hawkins is not one of our soldiers. He's an escaped prisoner."

The communication tech interrupted with a report, "Warden Seward, sir. I've just received a message from Captain Hawkins aboard the Hellion warship. It says, 'Jacob Seward, I am leaving now, but I hope someday to chance upon you once again.'"

10

MAN OF DESTINY

There was no question who the captain of the *Destiny* was—there was no vote or discussion, no argument or controversy, no persuasion or cajoling—every man who the day before had been a prisoner without hope and today was a free man with a future, knew who they would follow—the man who was at the forefront of the battle—Jamie Hawkins.

Captain Jamie Hawkins was seated in the command chair of the *Destiny* when Hale stepped onto the bridge and reported, "I've given the astrogator the coordinates of rebel base Echo."

Hawkins nodded. "Helm, set course for base Echo, ahead full."

"Aye, Captain."

"What now, Jamie?" asked Hale.

"What now, you ask?" said Hawkins jubilantly, spreading his arms wide to encompass the entire universe. "Now, we do as we please."

He watched as Zeno shrank to nothing on the view screen. *Freedom is delicious.*

Hawkins was not yet twenty seven years old, yet, he had served in combat for several years as a Marine, and now he was in command of a fine ship. He knew commanding a ship would to be different from other responsibilities he had known, but he did know how to handle men.

He stood at the head of the wardroom table, with his newly promoted officers around him. He placed his hands on his hips, and barked, "Ha! You've done it, you great lump of fools. I call you fools for attempting so foolhardy an assault in the face of such overwhelming odds, but most of all, you're fools for following the likes of me!"

Around the table the men roared with laughter and nodded their heads in agreement with every word. They knew all too well how foolish they had been, but they now had true faith in Hawkins. He could do no wrong in their eyes. He searched their faces, hoping to know them soon—their strengths and weaknesses. One of his strengths was his positive attitude which was infectious and lead to everyone thinking that whatever they faced, they could succeed.

The *Destiny* had a rocket-shaped hull. It was over two hundred meters long, equipped with a sub-light antimatter engine and thirty-six ray guns, half of which were medium caliber 24 gigajoule dark energy lasers capable of penetrating an enemy ship's shield and titanium steel hull. Lesser caliber guns were mounted as well for close range. The sensing equipment included several different types of active radars and passive telescopes. The spectrum of emissions was strictly controlled so that the ship would be difficult to detect when it operated at minimal power.

Looking around the spacious semicircular bridge, Hawkins shifted in his seat to get a better glimpse of his new home. He met the eager faces of the bridge crew with an approving eye.

Soon the *Destiny* was alive with bustling repair activities. The next few days flew by swiftly. It seemed that there were never enough hours in a day and he found himself delegating more and more responsibility to his executive officer, Aaron Hale.

For the first time, in a long time, Hawkins was satisfied. Later, he would determine the fate of the Hellion prisoners. But for now it was with excitement, curiosity, and impatience that he took the *Destiny* to Echo.

Hale knocked on the captain's stateroom door. Without waiting for a response, he entered and said, "We need to have a conversation about the rebellion."

Hawkins grimaced and replied, "We're escaping from prison, not founding a political movement. We've no infrastructure, or support, for an insurgency."

"You're a folk hero, thanks to the hospital episode. People will rally around you. Why do you think the government worked so hard to convict you and sentence you to Zeno? It was to get you out of the public eye."

"I have simple passions—a desire for love, a thirst for knowledge, and pity for the deplorable plight of mankind," declared Hawkins. "None of those compel me to start a revolution."

"It's already started. We just need to find the right leader. I think that might be you, but we don't have a great deal of time. Victor will mount an all-out effort to eliminate us. He'll hunt us down, in order to destroy the threat we represent to his foul government."

Hawkins felt a kinship with Hale, born of need and spirit, but they served separate goals and desires. Hale wanted to build and support a revolution while Hawkins was still narrowly defining his role in terms of escape and evade. Yet, they put a good face on their alliance. Someday, Hawkins hoped to profit from Victor's fall, but he was reluctant to predict when it would happen, or if he would be a part of it.

"I think you see our government as a sham, a farce acted out by hypocritical buffoons. For you, politics is the playground of the wicked."

"And you find redeeming value in the politics?" asked Hawkins.

Hale leaned forward closer to Hawkins' face and said, "Yes, when it's conducted with honesty and selflessness, it can serve the people."

"Hold on to those good thoughts—for I know you to be sincere—but allow me my doubts."

11

CAPTIVE

Hawkins slouched in a comfortable chair. After his prison cell, the captain's cabin felt spacious, even luxurious. The furnishings showcased the previous owner's preference for traditional military decor. He examined a desk in the corner. Several personal items were arranged orderly on the top, including an oil painting, a portrait of a young, attractive woman. He opened the draws and searched through the desk. Then he opened a trunk of personal possessions and rummaged through it for several minutes. He wasn't looking for anything in particular; rather he was seeking contact with the normalcy of existence—outside of prison.

A knock on the cabin door interrupted his woolgathering.

"Enter."

A disheveled Hellion officer was shoved in and forced into a chair across from him. The prisoner rubbed his hand over the lump on his head and looked around vacantly until his eyes focused on the swashbuckling figure in front of him, once more clad in a pilot jacket and boots.

"Who are you?"

"I'm Captain Hawkins, at your service, Lieutenant Connors. Forgive me, for having looked through the ship's documents, and for helping myself to some of your ship's civilian clothes. No doubt you're confused, but let me remind you: I am the one who hit you on the head and took possession of this fine ship."

Connors was not past thirty, but his balding head, sunken face, and beaked nose made him appear older. But his thickset body was broad and powerful. His long black mustache drooped into a frown. He sat upright, despite the discomfort written over his face.

"Allow me," said Hawkins, handing him a flask. "It's an alcoholic concoction I found aboard. I trust it will ease your discomfort and dull the pain."

Connors took a cautious sip. Recognizing it, he gulped down a long swallow. The vague embarrassment deepened into a scowl as his memory cleared. He stared at Hawkins from his green eyes, still somewhat bewildered.

Gesturing at the man's head, Hawkins asked, "Still aching?"

"Yes." Conner's disheveled clothes rustled against his chair, as he leaned his head back and drank heartily from the flask once more.

"Our medic examined you, and he assures me that other than a headache, you will completely recover by tomorrow."

"Who the devil are you to steal my ship?" His eyebrows furrowed and his lips curled.

"Don't torture yourself over your loss. It's merely the fortunes of war. This is now my ship and I've been helping myself to whatever I could find, and oh yes, your tasty thirst-quencher. What do you call it?"

"It's called quinto, a home grown concoction of vodka and tequila."

"I tried some. It packs quite a wallop."

The captain took another pull on the flask. He said, "What do you plan to do with me and my crew? Kill us?"

"I'm not unsympathetic to your plight, Lieutenant Connors, having recently suffered a similar ordeal and I can assure you that you will be treated as prisoners of war with all the formalities and rights that status affords," said Hawkins emphatically.

Elated surprise registered briefly on Connors' face, quickly followed by skepticism. "You don't really expect me to believe that."

"I don't expect you to believe anything I say. Nevertheless, I am telling the truth."

Connors fell perfectly silent and sat straight and stiff under Hawkins' scrutiny.

"I do have a few questions, however, that you could help me with if you've a mind to. It will also facilitate a more comfortable passage for you and your men, until we can arrange a prisoner exchange with your government."

"Questions? What questions?"

At ease and smiling, Hawkins said, "Nothing of military importance that would compromise your honor, I assure you. You see, my men and I are not in good standing with the Jaxon government. We were prisoners on the penal colony you so rudely intruded upon. Now we're rebels in their eyes. So our objectives may not be as dissimilar as you might first imagine."

"Ah," said Connors, relaxing his face into an expression of insolent amusement.

Hawkins said, "This war is being waged as something deeper than a mere dispute over territory—it is rooted in greed and hate. Year by year, soldiers and civilians alike, have paid the price for the evil choices of our leaders. Play fair with me, and provide some basic information about this ship, and the asteroid bases, to aid my survival, and you'll be treated well and offered for exchange to return to your home. Otherwise . . ."

"I don't think I like the way you put that. Indeed, I'm sure I don't. How can I trust a traitor to his nation to keep his word?"

No humor glinted in Hawkins's cold eyes now; his face was set and hard. "I'm sorry for that, but it is what it is. If you think the Jaxon soldiers on Zeno will treat you any better, I can arrange your release to them."

"Why don't you just threaten to kill me? Oh, that's right, you have questions that need answering," said

Connors spitefully. "If I answer your questions, you'll let me go?"

"I'm afraid, I can't promise that much immediately, but I will work for a prisoner exchange that will include you. I assume you would prefer to choose your own fate, rather than leave it to the tender mercies of the Zeno soldiers you just bombarded."

Connors' pale eyes widened in sudden fear, he said, "I hope, I am not mistaken to trust you—I accept your terms—ask your questions."

"Let's start by your telling me what you know of how this war started."

"You're joking. Everyone knows the story."

"I'd like to hear your version."

"My version is the true story."

"As you say," said Hawkins.

Connors hesitated moment, then he said, "Several of the large Jaxon Eureka Mining Colonies (EMC) were oppressing people of Hellion descent who were living among them. These colonies were wealthy, easily supplied, and numbered more than twenty thousand residents of which a few hundred were said to complain. The colonies were situated at the midpoint of the belt at the vortex of the most frequented trade routes. When the tormented people beseeched the Hellion government for relief, Chairman Herman Rusk demanded a referendum that would allow the intimidated parts of some colonies to become independent."

Hawkins nodded thoughtfully. Rusk was an arrogant, self-centered, isolationist bully, who enacted many restrictive laws, secret organizations, and harassed, intimidated, and imprisoned political activists and critics, in order to remain in power.

Connors said, "A referendum was held on four EMC colonies and a majority of 93 percent voted to secede from Jaxon and join Hellion. The referendum was unfairly declared as illegitimate by Jaxon because they claimed that Hellion soldiers infiltrated and occupied the colonies. My government denied that and said the only troops active in the colonies were local self-defense forces. However, Rusk declared that our troops would stand behind the colony's self-defense forces."

Chairman Rusk met with President Victor where he expressed a willingness to discuss the situation. Victor protested diplomatically at first, stating that Rusk had ordered his troops to seize four rich Jaxon mining colonies, and Victor demanded that Hellion stop supplying arms to the separatist fighters. He said Jaxon wanted a political compromise and promised the interests of Hellion-speaking people in those colonies would be respected.

Connors said, "Rusk signed a bill that led to the annexation of those colonies by Hellion."

Hawkins nodded and said, "President Victor was outraged and threatened to take back the colonies by force."

Rusk stated that the annexation of the colonies was a historic event that would not be reversed and he declared war on Jaxon. Many credited Rusk for reviving Hellion fortunes once the war started, by pulling Hellion out of the chaos of a financial collapse.

"Chairman Rusk is a great man," said Connors.

"As you say," said Hawkins, but he thought . . .

Rusk's crude brazen bloodthirsty aggression was a risky venture.

The war had been locked in stalemate for years, draining resources and lives while the leadership of each side remained safe at home, keeping the majority of their military power close at hand for protection.

"Do you have more questions?"

"Yes."

Before he was finished, Hawkins asked many questions about the *Destiny* and activities in the asteroids. Afterward Conner's was returned to a holding cell and Hawkins brooded over what he had learned.

He considered his life as a series of incidents, channeled along an improbable path. At every moment he faced a door—step through one way to the future, the other to the past, but always, he was standing at a threshold.

Where does this latest door lead?

12

PRESIDENT VICTOR

President Charles Victor pounded a fist on his mahogany desk and said, "Ordinary people lack the capacity for critical thinking. They always obey the loudest voice shouting in their ear." His straight- nose, prominent chin, and bushy eyebrows gave him an appearance of astuteness that his character didn't actually possess. His heavy paunch and large frame made him an imposing figure, but his sallow pitted skin, and the twitch around his mouth, destroyed any semblance of a distinguished pose. His expensive but ill-fitting suit strained across his swollen body, and the perpetual perspiration dripping down his forehead gave the appearance of discomfort.

Victor waited with Senator Wattles in his private office inside the President's residence to present the merits of his war strategy to the congressional leadership which was to convene in a few minutes. His raised heart rate and shortened breathe belied the apathy, inertia, and weariness that his face pretended. Not known to be a creative or deep thinker, he was, however, difficult to rattle. He usually advanced his argument through articulate use of persuasive rhetoric. The style and delivery of his message often overshadowed its content, or at least obfuscated those parts of it that were unfavorable to his position.

"To be truly convincing when you speak in public," said Victor, "it's absolutely essential that you believe every word you say."

"Even when you're lying?" Senator Wattles asked with a sneer.

"Especially when you're lying," said Victor, with his deep booming voice.

"That's absurd. In fact, it's an oxymoron."

Victor chuckled, "And yet it works. The greater the lie, and the more sincerely you tell it, the more people will believe it."

"But really, Mr. President, it's impossible for you to believe your own lie. You *know* it's a lie."

Nodding, Victor said in complete earnest, "It takes practice."

He listened to the unpleasant arrhythmic drumming of Wattle's fingers on the desk and wondered why he bothered to discuss important issues with this man. Wattles responded dutifully to orders and occasionally offered useful advice, but had very little fire in him. What little there was could only be stimulated by bribes, or sometimes threats. Victor said in a seductive tone, "We live in a world where emotion is more persuasive than logic."

"It's not important whether you employ emotion, or logic, only that you convince the governing body to support your plan," said Wattles. "They're still suspicious that the wealth you've shared is less than the fortune you've stolen."

"Let them speculate. And stop that finger tapping! Besides, I don't exactly keep detailed books."

"But how much wealth is enough?"

"Always a little more than anyone ever gets," chortled Victor.

"Seriously, we've taken so much; do we need more money?"

"It's not about the money. It was never the money," said Victor, shaking his head at the man's blinding stupidity. "Money is merely a way of keeping score. It's about winning—and I want to win."

Wattles smiled wanly.

In a burst of passion, Victor exclaimed again, "I want to win!"

The senator was taken aback at the outburst.

They stood quietly for a moment, each collecting himself, before Victor resumed, "Besides, I've never lost an argument in my life. If I think I'm losing," he laughed once more, "I simply switch sides."

"There can be no changing sides on this occasion."

"Don't worry, I was being facetious. However, if someone does make a persuasive counterargument, I'll have him quietly 'disappear.'"

Senator Wattles blanched—knowing that the last remark was not facetious. While he often resented the abuse Victor heaped upon him, he was not unaware that "disappear," could easily be applied to him.

"Mr. President, I . . . uh . . .,"

Victor resumed speaking words of ruthless bloodthirsty greed—without any semblance of honor—even toward his fellow thief, "When speaking to friends and colleagues, it's always best to try the truth, first. So I'll explain the payoff and my ability to deliver, and why it's actually the best option available. If that doesn't work, I'll appeal to their patriotism and lie about our need to support the troops. If that fails, then I'll resort to my old standby—I'll have one, or maybe two, of them taken out for a word in private. When they don't come back, it's amazing how agreeable the rest become."

The congressional leaders waited in the Blue Room. The ornate wooden wall panels, centuries-old chairs around the huge oval table, oil paintings by old masters, and ancient tapestries complemented the view from the tall windows. Everything about the oversized room with its vaulted ceiling made guests feel small, intimidated, and exposed—as Victor intended.

When President Victor strutted in, everyone rose and remained standing in uncomfortable silence while he took his place at the head of the table.

Victor waved them to their seats.

Secret Service agents stood around the room, while additional plain-clothes agents flanked the President's chair. A recent assassination attempt provided yet another opportunity for Victor to flaunt his status, even—or perhaps especially—in the President's inner sanctum.

Victor let the silence linger a moment longer, then in a solemn voice and without preamble, he intoned, "Today, we face two grave threats."

A paused added the dramatic effect, he sought. "Hellion has plagued us for several years, but thanks to the heroic efforts our brave soldiers, Hellion remains distant and managed—tense, but on a slow fuse."

He inspected each face, fixing every member of the council with a cold stare.

"But now we must confront a new, more insidious, existential threat."

SMACK!

His hand slapped the table. "A threat that strikes our very heart and soul—rebels—both on Jaxon and within the asteroid colonies. I'm going to tell you a story—a story of suspense and emotion of how I'm going to win the prize for us all, if you support my proposal. This may not be the easiest choice, but it's the one with the greatest payoff.

"The regrettable Newport violence has had grave consequences which are far reaching. It's given birth to serious resistance and caused some in the military to waiver. I regret to say, during the upheaval, some of our troops got out of hand and there were a few massacres, and one near massacre. We managed to suppress information and news about them, as much as reasonably possible. However, one story that has had a lot of play involves a former Marine, named Hawkins."

"Was it he, who intervened and prevented the massacre at the Newport hospital?" asked a congresswoman.

That was only a guess. But a good one, thought Victor.

He said, "The rebels have circulated that unfortunate rumor to drum up support. Hawkins' celebrity soared after he hijacked a Hellion warship and escaped from Zeno."

"Ah! Quite a rogue," the congresswoman exclaimed.

"Nothing of the kind," snapped Victor, and pounded his fist on the table again.

BAM! BAM!

"He's a disease, a cancer, a poison. And we must find the cure."

Victor waited to let that sink in.

He glared around the table once more before continuing, "I've placed a bounty on his head." Taking a deep breath, his voice dropped to a whisper, "The rebels are becoming more and more troublesome. You'll see from the briefing book that to eliminate them, I require a significant increase in my emergency discretionary account."

Their collective gasp caused him to pause. He would have liked to read their minds and discover which were privately plotting against him at that particular moment.

"What preparations have been made, in case of another full scale riot in Newport?" asked one congressman.

"I've brought an entire army division within the city limits."

"In the meantime, we must move the bulk of our wealth to a safer location," suggested another.

A murmur ran around the table.

Victor savored the few seconds of silence before one congressman said sharply, "You told us that a short, sharp war was just what we needed to distract the public while we enriched ourselves. But this war has lasted a decade, and looks like it will last another."

Again Victor heard a murmur, and felt a knot tighten in his gut.

He lowered his brow and said sternly, "It's not profitable to revisit those arguments."

The balance of power in the room was as uncertain as the state of the fragile Jaxon democracy. Many of the people's representatives took warning from Victor's tone and changed the subject, fearing that he had already crossed the line to absolute authority.

The Jaxon government faced strategic problems, the magnitude and complexity of which, were unparalleled in its history. The situation at the war front had recently taken a disastrous turn. The Combat Fleet commander, Admiral Forester, one of the few competent men in the Jaxon space navy, had been arrested and temporarily detained for challenging the government's violent behavior in the Newport carnage. He was later released when the Hellion military won a dazzling string of minor victories. While they were not decisive, they were disturbing.

Senator Wattles stood up and said, "Let me review our current war disposition. Our Home Fleet includes a hundred of our best ships along with space stations and planet fortresses for our protection. Our forward based Combat Fleet stationed at the edge of the frozen cold rocks of the asteroid field, numbers about fifty ships including half of our biggest and most powerful. Another fifty medium and small ships make up the Escort Fleet which patrols various shipping lanes and guards our two hundred and ninety-three mining colonies. Hellion has a similar number of colonies after stealing several of ours. A dozen of our colonies are leaning toward rebels and three are known to be outright rebel bases."

On paper, the Jaxon military equaled the opposing forces of Hellion. They could muster two hundred warships and several thousand support vessels. It reported an army of over three hundred thousand men in uniform. But in actuality, these forces were depleted in every aspect of military performance. There was no significant research and development program. The maintenance and supply organizations were mostly a sham. Over time, the experience of the troops improved their performance, but the training of replacements remained low. Nevertheless, the character and the raw fighting quality of the men remained high. The military bases, satellites, and fortresses were stripped of equipment to supply frontline units. There was inadequate firepower and obsolete equipment on the frontline units despite the superior manufacturing and industrial base of Jaxon. This dire situation was the result of corrupt politicians who syphoned defense money into their own pockets and manipulated the distribution of their heavy weapons. In addition, Jaxon's leaders tended to promote officers based on political expediency rather than performance.

"Our mineral cargos from the mines are being interrupted by raiders, both Hellion and rebel," commented a senator.

Victor said, "I propose funding and outfitting a new Special Forces Fleet. This force will occupy the dissenting colonies and destroy rebel strongholds and ships. The SFF's primary mission is to kill or capture rebel leaders, including the infamous Captain Hawkins."

Wattles said, "The rebel situation here on Jaxon is uncertain. Our spies are of dubious value, though we have identified a number of rebel leaders. Everything depends on this body agreeing to fund the Special Forces."

"We are having great difficulty financing the war because of theft," commented the newest congressman and instantly everyone tried to hide their guilty faces around the table.

"Surely, you don't believe that?"

"That's a frightening idea."

"What about taking our attention off the forward bases?"

Victor's discipline allowed him to withhold speaking aloud the curses that he thought. He bit his tongue instead. He looked around and felt their sense of panic.

An emotional storm had been brewing within Victor's mind, forcing a string of curses from his mouth before he could stop them.

"Our intelligence has gathered detailed information on the rebel and Hellion bases."

A clear musical chime sounded as his aid interrupted and entered the room with a message. He took the note and read it without absorbing its meaning. He let the general read it and sat quietly while he did.

Victor said, "The Escort Fleet had a battle on the frontier that ended in a draw. This is a disaster. We face a balance of power where one threat is quickly opposed by a counterthrust."

Wattles said, "But, it was indecisive."

"That's the disaster. If we had won this battle, we would have gained much, and if we lost, we could have used it to get more taxes from the people. But a draw means the war has not progressed one millimeter and the people will be, all the more, crying for my head," said Victor in a purely self-indulgent moment. Despite himself, the corners of his mouth twitched.

It took another hour of charming, coaxing, cajoling, flattering, and cursing, before Victor's performance won agreement to fund his Special Forces Fleet when he resorted to threatening each member of the committee, individually and collectively.

He could now implement a plan, that he felt sure would make him even wealthier than he had thought possible.

The whole problem was that it made sense on paper; it was the execution that was so questionable. That was the critical flaw. In theory, he could cede the point, but what then?

He spoke glibly, "The plan lacks a leader who can make it work. He must have the faith of his convictions. Who is capable of executing this plan, you ask?"

Again, a murmur passed around the table.

He asked again, his voice dripping with derision: "What man of you can do so?"

None replied. A malicious smile sealed his victory.

"I picked and prodded at this problem until one name came to mind—Anthony Rodríguez."

Victor sat in his private office with General Rodríguez standing at attention before him.

He leaned forward, pleasant and charming. "General, I have just come from a meeting with the congressional leaders where we've decided to implement your suggestion for a Special Forces Fleet. You will have overall military command of twenty warships and ten thousand soldiers. Your deputy will be Admiral Samuels."

For a moment, Rodríguez hardly reacted; ensconced in his own mental processes, he bowed his head slightly and said in a clear crisp voice, "Thank you, Mr. President. I will not disappoint you."

"I'm counting on you to stamp out all rebel resistance and, restore law and order in the mining colonies. The rebels are weak because they lack a strong leader, but if one emerges, he could be a rallying point. That's why I want this folk hero, Hawkins, found and eliminated. You were promoted for this mission, specifically because you have personal knowledge of him. I expect you to use that familiarity to bring him to justice."

Rodríguez stood silent and impassive.

Victor mused, "There's something dangerous about him, about the way he doesn't give a damn."

"I understand, Mr. President."

"I'm relying on that," said Victor, and a smile unfurled on his lips. You've exhibited more awareness, more initiative, than your contemporaries. People, including myself, are confident that you will continue to rise in rank...if you succeed in this mission."

Rodríguez smiled. It was not the insipid smile Victor usually saw on his sycophants. This was a dangerous smile—a predatory smile. Victor noted with amusement that it was not unlike his own.

This one bears watching.

Victor stood up, his smile suddenly gone. "One more thing; is there anything more on the assassination attempt against me?"

"Unfortunately the assassin died under interrogation. However, what we have learned suggests that he was a Hellion secret agent, not a rebel."

"Damn—the worst of all possible worlds. If he had been a rebel, we could have gotten some propaganda value out of the incident."

"According to our spies on Hellion, this attempt implies that their leadership is considering more drastic action. They might be suffering their own internal problems."

"I don't like the sound of that."

"We should give them a taste of their own medicine," Rodríguez suggested blandly.

Victor locked his hands behind his back and strolled to the window. Shaking his head he said, "Wrong move—that would only encourage further attempts. Instead, let's use this to our advantage. Put out the word that the assassination attempt was the work of rebels and strike against their local support groups, both here and in the colonies."

"That will drive them further underground."

"We have a good fix on at least several of their groups; round them up."

"Yes, Mr. President."

"Is there any evidence of collusion between the rebels and Hellion?"

"None of our intelligence services have been able to establish that, sir."

"Then find some, or make some. Do you understand?"

"Yes, Mr. President."

Victor paced around the room. "We should have acted more aggressively against the rebels, last year."

"We weren't prepared then, Mr. President. We're over-extended now, as it is."

Staring intently at Rodríguez, Victor said, "The stakes in this venture couldn't be higher—the life or death of our nation." Then he pointed his finger at Rodríguez and then to himself.

He paused and examined the general's face to see if he had extracted every last measure of commitment. He added, "In every crisis, there's an opportunity—make this yours."

"I will, Mr. President."

"A showdown with Hellion is coming and we must make it happen on our terms. We can't be tied down dealing with rebels. Is that clear?" asked Victor.

"You have my word, Mr. President. I will make it my mission to destroy Jamie Hawkins."

13

RUSH INTO DANGER

For a few blissful breaths, Hawkins lay on his cot, his eyes closed, relaxing just enough to think he might fall back to sleep, but no, the world around him demanded his attention. He should have known better than to expect he could remain undisturbed for a complete sleep cycle. He had already discovered what it meant to never get enough sleep, never to relax, never to enjoy the peace and quiet of his own thoughts. Disheveled and bleary eyed, he got up and went to the bridge.

It was an anxious moment.

As the *Destiny* approached rebel base Echo, a garbled transmission reported the rebel base was under siege from a Jaxon ground force, with warships bombarding it from orbit.

"Not the warm welcome we were expecting," said Hale, his lips twisting into a frown.

Hawkins ordered, "Helm, take us in from the far side so the Jaxon ships can't see us."

"Aye, Captain.

Like most small planetoid bodies, the Echo asteroid was too inhospitable to terraform. An elaborate titanium frame supported a structure that maintained a habitable environment for the colony of miners. A shield and nearby fortress offered limited protection from enemy forces, but their chief protection had always been secrecy. Once the Jaxon space navy knew the colony had become an active rebel base, it was only a matter of time before the inevitable happened.

"Gunny what's your assessment?"

Gunny looked up from this tactical display and said, "The three ships are medium frigates, each carrying thirty-six guns, half of which are medium twenty-four gigajoule dark-energy lasers. That means that each one of them is our equal. The fort is keeping them at maximum range with its ray guns, but Jaxon has landed a military assault force that has surrounded the fort. Their weapons on the ground have limited flexibility; they're designed to fire at ships in orbit and can't rotate far enough to protect their back. The rebels are badly outmanned and outgunned. The fort will probably fall within twenty-four hours."

Hale interjected, "They don't have much of a chance. The Jaxon soldiers have cut off the living quarters and seized a key position overlooking the fort."

Hawkins looked at the indicated position on a 3D map projection.

Hale said, "I know the base commander. I wouldn't be surprised if he was contemplating surrender. Allowing Jaxon troops to land was a serious blunder. The message said he launched a failed counterattack that incurred heavy losses. They're in a grim position."

Hawkins knew that if the rebels inside the fort were tearing each other apart with dissention, worse would follow. Events were moving rapidly and it required swift action on his part, if he is to consider intervening on the side of the rebels.

But what can I do with one ship and two hundred men?

Hale said, "We came here looking for sanctuary. That's no longer possible. We should withdraw before we're discovered."

Hawkins wavered.

I've been fighting this. Now, I must decide.

He inhaled and held his breath a few seconds—then he exhaled—slow and steady. He fixed his penetrating eyes on Hale and asked, "You're the one who championed revolution. Don't you want to fight for it—here and now?"

Hale took a step back and furrowed his brows. He stammered, "I . . ., but what can we do?"

A plan was already forming in Hawkins' quick, decisive mind: launch a land assault from the far side of the asteroid.

He said, "I think we could intervene and save that rebel base. If we act immediately before we're detected."

It's done! I'm a rebel.

Hawkins said, "I think a land assault has a chance, if it's carried off with élan. They wouldn't be expecting anything like that. We could catch them by surprise. If we start now, we can reach a drop point where we can land the assault force on the back side of the asteroid."

Pointing to a point on the 3D image of the asteroid's surface, he said, "A hundred men will make a good landing party at the base of this hill."

Gunny was less enthusiastic. "One hundred men—to break a siege of two thousand soldiers and three warships?" he asked doubtfully.

Ignoring the dissent, Hawkins said, "We can follow the crest of the hill along this path to the backside of the fort. At just before dawn, we attack the siege troops holding the ridge."

"You make it sound easy, but are a hundred men enough?" asked Hale.

"I think they just might do," said Hawkins. "The Jaxon can't have much more than that number on the ridge protecting their heavy weapons. What intelligence we've gleaned from the rebel's transmission indicates that most of the Jaxon soldiers are staked out in redoubts around the fortress and the rest are around the mining facilities."

Hale and Gunny exchanged glances of bewilderment.

Hawkins continued, "Once the ridge is in our hands, we can use their own weapons to drive off the siege force."

Hale's face looked pale. "Jamie, we've believed in you and followed you, but this is suicide. We'll throw away the lives of one hundred men."

"It's like cleaving a diamond," said Hawkins. "Turning a rough diamond into a faceted gem takes a precision strike—well executed—otherwise you shatter it and end up with a mess. On the other hand, a well-executed blow can produce a fabulous gem. This precision strike at the ridge is just what we need."

"What if the enemy doesn't do what you think? What if the rest of the soldiers don't withdraw?" asked Hale.

In the pause that followed, the throb of the ship's engines mimicked their own labored breathing.

Hawkins stood stock still. His mother had always said he ran headlong into danger, that he lacked the discipline and patience to solve difficult problems. That he failed to adequately express his stance. Now he needed to find his voice to convince his crew that his solution would work.

"It would be a military necessity to withdraw after losing such a key strategic position—and that's what they'll be faced with, once we take the ridge and aim their own heavy weapons down at them. There's no other response they can make once the siege is broken and the fort's guns are keeping their ships at bay."

"Damn, let's do it," said Gunny.

"I'm for it," said Mitchel.

"Hawkins will you lead the assault, or remain on board?" asked Hale, accepting the judgment of his colleagues.

"My place is at the head of the assault."

"Then let's lay out the logistics."

Hawkins sent a message to the rebel base, telling them to hold on, help was on the way, and conveying the gist of his ambitious plans.

While these events played out, Hawkins set about moving his ship to an advantageous position.

As they approached the asteroid, the communications tech said, "Captain, the Jaxon ships are jamming all signals."

Hawkins looked at the sensor screens. The Jaxon warships, several transport, and supply ships were in low synchronous orbit over the fort. The fort was nearly surrounded by a high mountain ridge. The ridge was the dominating geologic feature. Heavy mobile batteries were firing from the ridge onto the fort without the fort being able to return much counter fire and the fort's shields were weakening.

Hawkins hammered home that seizing the ridge was key to reversing their fortunes. There were soldiers in emplacements around the fort, but only one to two hundred on the key ridge position. He would assault the ridge with a mere hundred men and a dozen mobile cannon, but the element of surprise would greatly help their efforts. Once he took the ridge, the entire landing force would be vulnerable. Then the fort with *Destiny's* help could drive the enemy ships away.

Though obviously disappointed at not being part of the assault team, Hale was eager to command the ship during the action.

Hawkins ordered, "I need you to make a feint with the *Destiny* during the dawn attack to distract the defenders and hold their men at their stations."

Soon, half of the *Destiny* crew shuttled down, unobserved, to the opposite side of the asteroid from the fort.

Hawkins and his one hundred man army were scattered about the hillside dragging their small mobile weapons behind several tracked crawling vehicles. The men carried backpacks with all the food, water, ammunition, and medical aids that would have to last until they won the battle. There were no other vehicles; everyone had to wobble in the low gravity over the rough terrain to their destination which was to take six hours.

Though they formed a sorry picture, as troops go, Hawkins had confidence in his fierce fighters. A rough semblance of order began to emerge as they straggled along the trail.

In a remarkably short time, they were marching behind Hawkins' boundless energy. His training and experience taught him that his personal example and involvement was needed in every aspect of this mission, if it were to succeed. He went from man to man encouraging each in turn. He checked their readiness and asked many to repeat their orders to ensure they understood what they were about to do. They responded to the standard he set.

He dispatched one scout to travel below the ridge and another farther off to the other side. He had the dark shadow of the asteroid and the enemy's distraction on their own front, to hide their movements.

Hawkins was in the lead scouting the way while Gunny brought up the rear hurrying any stragglers along.

A dark figure, bouncing slightly in the low gravity, appeared before Hawkins.

"Everyone's landed and moving, Captain," reported Joshua.

"OK," he said, "I'll go ahead with an advanced party. You tell Gunny to keep the main body together and moving. Everyman is to keep in sight of the man ahead of him."

"Will do, Captain."

"Don't get distracted and lost in the dark. This is rough country."

It was a long climb from the shuttle landing strip to the top of the ridgeline that they had to follow to the fort. It was full of jagged and irregular shaped rocks and boulders. There were numerous cases of someone slipping and falling. Several had to be left behind on the trail. They would be attended to after the action. Until then, they could wait. Some let yells slip when they fell and that drew a sharp rebuke.

Hawkins set off with an advanced party of four, disappearing ahead of the rest into the dark. He heard muffled reports over his communication channel and admonished, "No talking, or signaling, unless absolutely necessary. Only use secure short range channels."

Joshua and Gunny chide the men to keep together and keep moving.

Only a few of Hawkins men were in armored suits, most were dressed only in pressure suits, and carried light weapons. The few mobile weapons were pulled along behind the column and moved with difficulty over the rugged ridge terrain. There brought only minimal supplies and food, just enough to last for half a day. They expected to get everything they needed after they relieved the fort. The foot journey over the gullies and small valleys was made more difficult by the dust and sand that made their footing less secure. The minimal brightness of the star background was barely enough to guide their way. They dared not use any lights of their own for fear of giving their position away.

At one point, Joshua caught up with Hawkins, once more, and said, "The main party is closed up and a quarter kilometer behind you, Captain. Four men have been left behind due to injury or equipment malfunction."

"Very well," said Hawkins. "Report back to Gunny. Tell him that we are within a kilometer of the fort and this will be our final jumping off line, at dawn. Tell him to come and fill in the line."

Hawkins left the advanced party at that point, to mark the way, and he went ahead, alone, to scout the ridge perimeter closer to the enemy outposts. He moved stealthily and observed the defenders and their breastworks, as well as several lookouts. They were focused on the fort, he noticed, and not paying attention to their rear.

Since he was wearing a pressure suit with a Jaxon uniform insignia that he had salvaged from the *Destiny's* previous owners, he decided to literally walk up to the Jaxon outpost and talk to the very soldiers, he'd been spying on.

He switched his communicator to the local short range Jaxon frequency.

At the edge of the mountain ridge, one soldier was looking down at the rebel fort through night goggles. From a spot one hundred meters behind him, Hawkins stood up in the dark and began walking calmly toward the man.

He approached to within five meters and then barked, "Soldier! Is this how you stand your post?"

Startled, the soldier turned around and raised his weapon.

Hawkins threw his chest out and put his hands on his hips and said, "Fool, if I was the enemy, you'd be dead already."

Stunned, the soldier was unable to speak.

Hawkins said, "Where is your teammate? There should be two of you standing this post."

Now the soldier blanched. He said, "Joe's in the tent. I think he's asleep."

"You have five seconds to get him up and out here, before I bring you both up on charges for dereliction of duty."

When Joe joined his buddy, standing before Hawkins, who to all appearances resembled a sergeant of the guard, they hemmed and hawed, and stammered and fumbled, their way through half a dozen excuses for their failure to maintain a proper guard.

Hawkins let them sweat for several more minutes before he said, "You seem like good men. You've made a mistake, but I've found that good men learn from their mistakes. So, I'm not going to put you on report."

They were so relieved that they fawned over Hawkins in gratitude.

He made a show of relaxing and asked if they had any refreshments. Looking guilty again, they produced a bottle of an alcoholic mixture which they shared. Soon, Hawkins was treating them like his own men. He chatted with them about soldiers' common gripes, and then about the progress of the battle. Soon he was talking about position assignments and movement timetables. He learned a great deal about the vulnerabilities of the ridge position.

Finally, he said, "I've got to move along and check the rest of the positions, but I expect you to remain alert from now on. If I come back don't let me catch you asleep again."

"Yes, sergeant, absolutely, you can count on us."

When Hawkins returned to his own men, he deployed them to take advantage of the new information he had gathered.

Joshua said, "You should not have taken such a risk, Captain."

Hawkins laughed, "I stuck my nose in and learned enough to make it worthwhile. They are planning an overland assault of the fort in mere hours. Our attack will not only forestall their plans, it will catch them off balance just when they are about to leave their trenches. It'll all work out splendidly."

He gave the final orders as the men prepared for their assault on the ridge. They remained hidden from detection in a gully while the final minutes ticked away.

He took a moment to appreciate how Joshua had matured and developed since their escape from Zeno.

He's become an energetic and resourceful aid.

In the pre-dawn glimmer, the men settled into position for the assault on the ridge. They crouched out of sight in a deep gully, restless but poised and ready.

As the first rays of light crested over the horizon with the asteroid's rotation, Hawkins's guttural command ran through the men:

"Prepare to attack."

But some men were already stirring and advancing.

Hawkins rose and running forward, he shouted, "Charge."

Together amass, the men emerged from the gully and started to storm the ridge redoubts. The unnerving dark was finally broken by a series of bright noisy explosions.

Hawkins wanted the assault to strike the defense as a single wave, but it turned out to be a ragged disorganized line when it actually reached the outer perimeter. The men were out of breath and fumbling to break into the redoubts.

The Jaxon soldiers in their entrenched siege positions did not raise the alarm until Hawkins and some men had already breached the first defensive trench.

"All together now," Hawkins bellowed over his communication channel.

They pushed together, breaking through as the inner barrier cracked open under the explosive onslaught.

Attacking a steep, narrow ridge defended by entrenched soldiers with heavy weapons may have seemed an impossible task, but defending that ridge from a surprise attack proved even more impossible. The attack opened with a stunning charge of the entire one hundred men launching themselves at the trenches. Several lead officers and men fell from the ragged defensive fire. The defenders fought stubbornly, but after suffering numerous casualties they began abandoning the ridge. Hawkins was in the thick of the action and was twice nicked by shrapnel. He was only saved by the suit's self-sealing pressurization feature.

The trenches extended underground, but the aboveground portion had several observation towers and three visible entrances. At each corner of the ridge they had a guard. Hawkins and several men moved between several of the smaller structures. He reached the entrance of one observation tower. Video and electronic surveillance could not easily see past his camouflage gear, but he was more concerned about his limited oxygen supply. As he entered the tower entrance, several guards spotted him. He grabbed the first one and threw him into the second. He ducked the swinging rifle butt of the third guard, and punched him in his midsection, doubling him over.

The battle was now inside the underground trenches and the towers. Laser beams flashed by, but only a trickle of men had penetrated the position, so far. Hand to hand combat ensued. Some groups were not as successful as the men with Hawkins. They fought some soldiers at the central tower position.

"Stand firm! Stand firm, you rabble," an officer screamed at his disintegrating troops.

At that, the Jaxon troops rallied and nearly turned the tide. Only a personal assault by Hawkins into the thick of battle restored the situation. Hawkins broke through the last Jaxon redoubt position almost singlehandedly.

Seeing a soldier aiming directly at him, Hawkins ducked behind a boulder and crawled forward in a trench. He let loose a few shots at an exposed Jaxon, and then charged straight at a second group of soldiers. About sixty meters away, there were several enemy soldiers. When he reached the end of the ledge, he fired again. He crawled forward toward the sound of more firing. Throwing grenades every few meters, he crept forward, making for better cover behind a mound. The unnerving dark was finally broken by a series of bright noisy explosions.

The flashes of plasma weapons shrieked past him, disintegrating a nearby rock.

What's happening?

Breathlessly, he shrank behind a bolder.

Dark swooping shadows wheeled toward him on the left. He didn't wait for the onslaught but rose to meet it, firing as rapidly as he could. The clash of their meeting erupted in white fury and burning hot plasma.

His breathing was now rapid and labored.

When he reached the heavy weapons, he began firing at vague figures in the dark. They tossed a grenade, and the flash of light gave him a chance to get his bearings. Looking away, he stumbled in the treacherous footing, sprang up, and sprawled back down across the ground. Regaining his feet, he continued his retreat toward sanctuary. Blinding flashes of plasma weapons again streaked past him, leaving smoldering displays of fireworks as they ricocheted off the rocks.

Gasping for air, Hawkins realized that his oxygen was running low. Amid all the confusion, the shouting, and the erratic motion, he couldn't distinguish the shimmers in his flickering vision from the plasma flashes and grenade explosions. He drew a deep breath, trying to stabilize the oxygen flow, and his sight cleared.

He blinked: he was surrounded!

They were his men.

As the rest of Hawkins' men surged over the ridge, the Jaxon troops began to lose heart. Some scrambled past each other, pushing and shoving, to reach the safety of the lower siege positions, not caring at all for their own wounded.

Soon positions were being secured.

Hawkins set up guards on important points and gathered the prisoners.

The Jaxon force, fearing that they would be bombarded from the ridge with their own heavy weapons, began a rapid retreat to their disembarkation point and exited the asteroid, just as Hawkins had predicted.

Soon, the entire attack force beat a path back to Jaxon.

Hawkins didn't interfere with the Jaxon withdrawal and let them retreat at their own pace. When the fortress was uncovered, he entered and resupplied his men. His gaze shifted to the fugitives from the battle, the injured and weary men staggering past.

Confronted by Hawkins, the local rebel base commander made the difficult decision to evacuate and moved his headquarters to a new location, but as they prepared to leave, Hawkins found himself embroiled in an internal power struggle over leadership.

14

SPECIAL FORCES

On the same day he took command of Special Forces, General Anthony Rodríguez learned that Hawkins had forced the withdrawal of all Jaxon forces from the mining colony on an asteroid named Echo.

With a flurry of initiative and energy, he led ten warships, half of the Special Forces Fleet, to Echo. Only after landing two thousand soldiers and seizing the fortress, did he discover that the entire mining colony and all its facilities had been abandoned. Hawkins and the rebels had vanished.

He cursed.

So close!

He was disappointed, frustrated, and worried about President Victor's "encouragement." Failure was unacceptable.

"We need to know where he's going, not where he's been. There's too much space with too few ships to cover it," Rodríguez ranted to his senior staff.

However, he remained focused and ordered, "Admiral Samuels, dispatch scout ships and drones throughout this quadrant to look for the rebel forces."

"Aye aye, sir."

But over the next few days, they found no trace of Hawkins, his ship, or anyone willing to talk about him. That did not mean he could stop pursuing every lead, especially considering Victor's last message.

Rodríguez concentrated on what he did know—the remaining colonies that were of questionable loyalty in the area. He made a list of possibilities and began crossing them off as intelligence was acquired. After a week, he had eliminated quite a few locations, and while he had a shorter list, his problem remained just as unsolved as before. There were simply too many incomplete and fruitless paths to pursue. He reached a vague sense of futility.

"He'll make a mistake," he said to himself, trying to muster his patience, "and I'll be ready."

At Admiral Samuels' suggestion, Rodríguez deployed a half dozen decoy ships, to pose as derelicts Q-ship that sat near important trade routes. Each Q-ship had a frigate nearby in quiet mode to swoop down if a rebel took the bait. However, the 'derelict' Q-ships were far from helpless. They had hastily constructed false hulls built to cover newly added rows of hidden weapons. When a rebel was snared, the Q-ship and its stealthy frigate would work together to destroy their victim.

A week later, alongside a solitary asteroid, a drone floated with only passive sensors and minimal emissions. It was nearly impossible to detect. It was listening, watching, and probing the black vastness of the belt. For a long time, not the faintest rebel emission illuminated its scanner.

Then it happened. A suspect signal popped up.

Soon another drone joined it, to gather information on the rebel. Then the picket reported a problem, the rebel was on a divergent course that the nearest Jaxon ship could not intercept without going to high power and revealing its position. It was decision time.

A frigate collected the drone's information and moved closer. It detected distant energy sources betraying unknown ships farther way. A tap of the engine power sent the frigate to investigate the new comers. The watching frigate counted the enemy units. It adjusted the finicky sensor strength and sent a burst transmission to its flagship, a frigate with Rodríguez aboard. It wasn't necessary to acknowledge the transmission, but it was necessary to update the drone's orders and return it to waiting. They could continue to hover and wait like a spider, or leap at the prey like a tiger, and hope to catch the rebel ship before it escaped.

Rodríguez decided to wait and draw more resources closer to the cluster of rebel cargo ships. The ambush was set. He was patient. His time would come. He didn't intend to spring the trap until he had all he could inside, as well as enough strength to haul them in.

When the optimal moment came, he pounced, however, the rebel cargo ships reacting more quickly than he had anticipated, scattered in all directions.

Rodríguez pulled ahead of one quarry by anticipating their course. He fired several shots as his target twisted desperately trying to evade, but the initial shots were telling. The wounded ship belched debris wreckage.

When the brief action was over, Rodríguez had managed to capture a single rebel freighter.

Nevertheless, that was enough for the trap to prove the concept of 'watch, wait, and leap.'

More traps would be set.

15

SPINDRIFT

Like a scruffy unkempt scarecrow, Ichabod Merrick was tall and lanky with large floppy ears and a bulbous beaked nose. His poor posture and hang-dog drooping face helped to make him an object of some amusement. And despite Hawkins' best efforts to be on good behavior, he couldn't help chuckling whenever Merrick's distracting singsong speech pattern emerged during the meeting.

Hale chastised Hawkins with a stern forbidding stare before he turned to Merrick and said, "Base Commander, I want to congratulate you on successfully transferring your headquarters and personnel from Echo to this asteroid, you've named Spindrift."

In his lyrical voice, Merrick said, "Thank you, Mr. Hale."

Inside the temporary shelter they had erected on Spindrift, the rebel leaders meet to discuss their future.

Merrick added, "Spindrift is remote with no mining colony within a million kilometers, so it'll be hard for our enemies to find this uncharted hunk of granite and ice. Unfortunately, it will be equally difficult to construct living quarters and support facilities on such a far-flung desolate rock."

Hale said, "A base is not just, so many buildings, people, and things, it's a pattern of higher organization, a blueprint for living in space. The asteroid field varies in density. Some clusters of asteroids will block radar signals to help keep us hidden."

Merrick said with unconcealed pride, "When we complete this colony, it will be powered by solar energy and we'll use thin-walled pressure vessels with recycled atmospheres and hydroponics. Each sector of our space habitat will have its own atmosphere control system with sensors and regulators including activated carbon filters and air ionizers."

Hawkins asked, "What's your timetable to complete construction?"

"We'll have temporary shelter and basic services up within two weeks. After that we'll upgrade the construction to full service within two months."

Hawkins said, "We must move as fast as possible. Our enemies could discover us at any time and each day is precious in building our strength and finding additional people and resources."

Merrick spent nearly an hour, disgorging all the information he had on asteroid commerce, before Hawkins interrupted and said, "I want to thank you for that briefing on operations within the asteroid belt. If I understand the gist, there are several thousand commerce vessels in the inner half of the star system and a like number beyond the asteroids. They service nearly a thousand mining colonies which transport mineral wealth to their respective governments and they are in turn resupplied with food, equipment, and finished goods."

"That's right," said Merrick. "To safeguard commerce within the inner planets the Jaxon navy has about fifty medium and small warships in their Escort Fleet while Hellion has about an equal number to protect the outer planets' commerce."

"That's not counting the Home and Combat Fleets of each side which are not likely to pay much attention to us," said Hawkins.

Merrick continued, "That's right. Against these numbers, we can muster three converted cargo vessels with a few small weapons and a half a dozen transport ships to move forces about. Oh, and then there's your frigate, the *Destiny*—our only actual warship. In addition, there are a few scattered rebel bases in the asteroids and a few groups of rebel supporters on Jaxon itself."

It was apparent to all that the lack of a space navy was problematic for a revolution. Even the few ships they did have, had been hijacked from the enemy. Some merchant ships could be lightly armed as well, but since the rebels were greatly outnumbered and outgunned, such ships would have to be used wisely. They needed a commander to motivate and deploy them. Most rebel officers were of dubious combat potential with the exception of those aboard the *Destiny*.

Hawkins folded his hands tight before him. He recognized that the seat of rebel power was on Jaxon, but this base represented their main military force in the asteroids—such as it was. He had no formal negotiating training and could only rely on his own experience to guide him, but his instincts told him that this base commander was ill-suited for his position.

Hawkins asked, "I presume you will support my efforts and supply my ship?"

"You presume a great deal, perhaps too much," said Merrick whose previous experience as a warehouse manager made him prone to hoarding. "But let's proceed slowly, shall we?"

"What other prospects have we? We're outlaws," laughed Hale.

"Yes, but we've chosen our enemies with discrimination—the governments of Rusk and Victor," laughed Hawkins. "And we can attack them with discrimination, as well."

"Do you know how much, the people hate Victor?" asked the base commander. "How much, they really hate him? Not just a little, but actively and intently. How long they have lived in fear of him and his police thugs."

"Our people are divided by this government. The only thing we all have in common is the misery Victor has caused," said Hale.

"Unfortunately, the public is thoroughly disgusted, not only with the Victor administration, but they are angry with the rebels who led them into violent defeat, such as the disaster at Newport," said Hawkins waiting for the reaction he knew would come.

He watched Merrick's face for a reaction, and was not disappointed. Hawkins could see that there was as much internal strife and dissent within the rebel organization, as ever.

I've got to win this man over.

Hawkins said, "I propose we avoid attacking Jaxon military bases because that would assist the Hellion. Instead we will target Hellion ships and bases and take equipment and weapons from them. However, to punish the Jaxon government, as well, we will raid their gem and mineral shipments that line their personal pockets. It may undermine their ability to stay in power."

"That seems overly ambitious," said Merrick, nevertheless warming to the possibility.

Hawkins said, "A well-handled small force can appear more formidable by striking strategically and winning small tactical victories—which I intend to do—with your support. Of course, I plan to bring all the booty and goods we acquire, here for you, to keep and distribute to our rebel friends."

A great smile emerged on Merrick's face for the first time. He clearly liked the thought of vast quantities of materials and goods coming into his possession to hoard and distribute at his discretion.

Merrick said, "You should know that Victor has your face plastered over the tele. Your anonymity is at an end. He has sent people to hunt you down and kill you."

"They'll have to find me first."

Hawkins knew that exploiting his success of escaping Zeno, and proclaiming it a rebel victory, would yield dividends and stop panic-stricken fears. He publicly praised Hale and the rebels who followed him, and raised their profile while tamping down opposition voices. He made contact with news reporters, he could trust, to get his words to the Jaxon public and he even began talking about a rebel government in exile. This immediately got resonance. He seemed a colorful warrior that could rescue them. There were those who thought him a great man, but he was not one of them. He held himself in less regard. He recognized that his public popularity was being exploited by some, while others saw him as a threat.

The base commander said, "I'm not in a position to plan a rebellion that can change the Jaxon government."

"Then who is?" asked Hawkins.

"Only the rebel groups united under Catherine Parker on Jaxon have the loyalty and reach to even consider such an option."

Hawkins hated to leave problems unsolved, but some would have to wait until he could meet with Parker. Then more out of obstinacy, than a sincere intent to get things organized, he went back to work, sorting out solutions that *were* within his grasp.

Hawkins went around the table, pointing to individuals as he spoke, "You: Prepare a list of all personnel on this base, their duties and responsibilities. You: Inventory all equipment including weapons and their functionality. You: Work out what we will need to turn this base into a self-sustaining colony. You: Gather a list of the nearest mining colonies whose leaders might be willing to make black-market deals. You: Get intelligence on the Miramar bases and their defenses to see which ones might be vulnerable to raids. You: Find out when and where convoys are scheduled to pass through this area. One way or another, we will stand up and be noticed."

16

MIXED SIGNALS

For a man who had never commanded more than a company of Marines in combat, Hawkins demonstrated advanced military tactics and imaginative initiative by juxtaposing careful calculation with aggressive abandon. He moved among his men praising, encouraging, ordering, and scoffing. Their successes, though small, transformed a collection of misfits into enthusiastic, hard-charging warriors that knew they would always find him at the forefront of any danger they faced.

Hawkins enjoyed the comradery by having his officers visit him informally in his stateroom. He kept fresh snacks available which worked wonders in motivating them to return.

One day, there was a knock on his stateroom door. "Enter."

A young head peeked in and said, "Captain, I'm sorry to disturb you, but I have an update on the information you asked for."

"Come in, Joshua. Sit down."

Joshua said, "The data techs in CIC helped me compile a detail evaluation of the known Jaxon and Hellion bases in the asteroids."

He handed over his tablet.

"I see from your report that enemy ships and resources seem particularly high in the Alpha sector. Knowing how sensitive the enemy is to threats to their supply line, I've forced them to station ships in these rear areas by making feints at nearby bases. That has drawn away forces and may have left us an opening," said Hawkins, looking up from the datasheet.

"Yes, Captain. I've indicated the best targets," said the boy with a broad smile.

"I see that, but you neglected to identify the major threats that accompany those opportunities."

Crestfallen, Joshua quickly took back the tablet. He scrolled to a new page and showed Hawkins.

"I've tabulated the ship deployments. Here," he pointed.

Hawkins scrolled through some of the report's information about ship and soldier placements.

He said, "One of our major tactical challenges has been to safely cross the large expanse of the belt to reach a position from which we can launch an attack. Your information will help. Well done."

Joshua beamed.

For the last month, Hawkins had made a series of swift raids—widely dispersed to conceal any pattern to rebel movements—that had yielded meaningful plunder. But they had a secondary purpose as well. "Did you find any patterns in Jaxon fleet movements?" he asked.

"I did," said Joshua eager to explain his insight. "The Jaxon navy is collecting forces at their main base. It's possible that they intend to make a broad sweep through the asteroid belt to ferret out rebels—and from all indications, they could strike soon."

Hawkins considered the evidence.

Joshua added sheepishly, "Actually, it was the data techs in CIC who pointed that out to me."

Hawkins nodded and said, "I intend to disrupt their plans by striking first and leading them on a merry chase. I think we can make a good diversion, if carried it out aggressively. It could throw them off balance and give us the time we need. Let me point out to you that we are greatly outnumbered and we severely lack men and material. No amount of clever maneuver, or bold action, is enough to compensate for such weaknesses indefinitely, at some point, we must get stronger."

"How?"

In a distracted manner, Hawkins mused, "The logistic issues are beyond difficult, considering our merger resources; we're desperately short of skilled soldiers, heavy weapons, and ships. Where will more come from?"

"Well sir, the defeats the Hellion military have suffered has motivated them to send ships after us and you've managed to capture several."

"Ha!" laughed Hawkins. "I don't think encouraging Jaxon and Hellion to send more ships after us is the right solution to growing our fleet. We've been lucky so far. They chose aggressive officers who proved that they were not up to the task. They divided their force and tried to spread an inadequate net to trap us."

"Yes, Captain, but your unorthodox tactics have given us victories."

It was true that Hawkins had used intricate successful maneuvers, both militarily and diplomatically. His goal was to always limit his opposition's moves while maximizing his freedom of movement.

So far, his enemies had not divined his strategy—a task that required a sharper mind than Victor's. And because Victor had to both check the rebel unrest, and battle the Hellion at the same time, he often made muddled or wrong moves. All the dark pageantry of politics and war could not compare with Hawkins' personal leadership. He was proving to be a more resourceful and energetic leader, than they could cope with.

Hawkins said, "It's true that our military successes have enabled us to make alliances with several colony base commanders to get information and supplies in exchange for our plunder. I've found that acquiring mineral ores allowed us to buy support from those who were otherwise less inclined toward the rebellion.

My favorite deal was with the financial money men on Jaxon who were willing to hedge their bet against the Victor government."

Joshua asked, "Despite everything you've done, do you really feel we have a chance against such enormous numbers?"

Hawkins frowned and said, "I believe that it is better to fail, than not to try.

Joshua remained sitting quietly for several minutes.

"Was there something more you wanted to talk about, Joshua?"

The boy whispered, "Yes."

Hawkins waited.

"I think I've found something important, but it may be nothing. The tech told me to forget it, but I . . ., I don't know, it bothers me."

"Tell me and let me decide," said Hawkins sympathetically.

"Sir, I was working with the data techs, trying to analyze the communication patterns of the Hellion fleet," said Joshua, licking his dry lips, excitedly. "And I've come across a very unusual signal."

Hawkins gave him an encouraging nod.

"It was a burst of radio signals from deep space. I traced it to either a 4 billion-year-old star in a constellation 44.4 light years away, or to another star in that same constellation, but much farther away. That means that the radio waves have been travelling to us for at least forty-four point four years."

Hawkins said, "Deep space radio signals have many plausible explanations—radio interference from planets, or rogue signals caused by local planet microwave devices. Another possibility could be stellar flares which can produce a one-time powerful signal. Even a pair of comets could be a source.

"That's true, Captain. That's what the techs said. They said, it could be just the effect of a natural space object, like a pulsating quasar, but it's also possible . . . I think maybe . . . it could be a message from another civilization."

Now smiling broadly, Hawkins said, "Given the unlikelihood of that, why are you concerned?"

"Because it was not a one-off event," said Joshua excitedly and then pausing to catch his breath. "I've recorded a half dozen repeating signals from the exact same source."

Nodding, Hawkins said, "That's a little more interesting, but an explanation for that could be a lighthouse-like rotating stellar pulsar with the signal sweeping in frequency."

"But Captain, the implications could be mind-blowing. Imagine, what if it was an alien civilization, and they were far more advanced than us, and they were trying to make contact? After centuries of fruitlessly scanning the stars and finding no evidence that anyone else is out there, this could be . . . could be . . ."

Joshua became paralyzed by his own imagination.

"Joshua, even if this signal were not natural, it might still be the product of one of Earth's colonies—not aliens."

"No sir, I've checked. There were no Earth colonies in the vicinity of the signal's star cluster when we last had contact with Earth, fifty years ago," said Joshua. Then in a rush of words, as he was apt to do, he spewed out, "And if there was a new colony since then, they couldn't have landed and set up their civilization and begun transmitting to us in less than the forty four years that signal has been traveling."

"Still you should curb your enthusiasm. There are many different possible explanations for what caused that signal—even a repeating signal—that we would have to rule out before we cry 'alien.' Signals like this have also been picked up before and none has panned out."

Joshua blinked and opened and closed his mouth several times, as if he wanted to argue further, but he couldn't offer any additional proof for his cause.

Hawkins said, "I agree, we should continue to monitor this frequency, but for now, it'll have to remain a mystery."

17

MASQUERADE

Commerce was the lifeblood of the Jaxon civilization and the shipping routes between its mining colonies and the inner planets offered Hawkins an opportunity to conduct raids to obtain new resources while harassing his enemy. The *Destiny* trekked through the asteroid belt to a key transit point where mineral freighters traveled. There she waited for a likely prospect. It wasn't long before they heard a distant emergency distress call.

SOS! SOS! SOS!

The comm tech tried to contact the ship, but there was no response.

Hawkins maneuvered the *Destiny* closer to the source of the call. When they had the ship on radar they decelerated to match the vessel's velocity. The ship looked like a derelict drifting near the shipping lanes.

Astrogator Williams scratched his head and said, "Something doesn't look right about that ship. Its profile seems strange and their SOS keeps repeating, but no one is responding to our messages."

"We don't know how long the distress has been broadcast. They might have abandoned ship and be far away, in escape pods," said Hale.

Williams said, "It looks too easy."

Hawkins ordered a medical rescue team to prepare to board the derelict and help any injured people. In addition, he prepared a team of engineers and damage control personnel to repair whatever had gone wrong with the ship's engines.

The derelict continued to transmit,

SOS! SOS! SOS!

"What do you propose?" asked Hale.

"Hale, you take command of the *Destiny*," said Hawkins. "I'm going to board the derelict and take a look,"

He ordered the comm tech to transmit a message to the derelict stating that a boarding party was coming to their aid with medical and engineering teams.

He loaded two shuttles with his rescue including Mitchel and Williams and approached the derelict.

There was no reply from the dead ship when the shuttle reached her. When they docked, Hawkins and his men opened the entry port hatch and boarded.

They entered the ship, but there was no one to greet them. Hawkins sent Mitchel with half the men to engineering while he led Williams and the others to the bridge. They looked to see if there were any injured as they proceeded, but found none.

Hawkins was only half way to the bridge when gunfire erupted, driving him and his men into a side compartment that boxcd them in with no exits and limited cover.

It's a trap. I've blundered into a trap.

Without wasting a moment, Hawkins began directing the firefight. He called, "Gunny, we're taking fire forward. We're in a precarious position."

"We're taking fire in engineering, as well, Captain," was the reply.

Hawkins men fought fiercely despite having had only their handguns against their opponent's battle armor and heavy rifles.

Notwithstanding the advantages of a prearranged trap, the Q-ship's Special Forces hadn't expected to face such a tough crew. They found progress difficult.

Over the din of battle, William's harsh querulous voice could be heard, "I warned you that this was suspicious—too easy. Now we're trapped. How're we going to get out?"

Hawkins scolded himself just as passionately. He, too, wondered how they would get out.

He had his men lay down covering fire while he and a few others tried to rush the one hatch in the compartment. The breakout attempt confirmed that they were surrounded and heavily outgunned—the fight was vicious and terrible—they were taking causalities without accomplishing anything. They fell back into the depths of the compartment.

Hawkins had to admit there was nothing more they could do. He called, "Gunny can you fight your way forward to help us."

"Captain, I'll try, but I think it's more of a case of you coming to get us."

I've led my men into ruin.

The Special Forces had the two groups of rebels isolated and pinned into small compartments without room for maneuver.

Hawkins contacted the *Destiny*, "We've been ambushed. Bring the *Destiny* closer and send reinforcements."

However, before these plans could be executed, the second element of the Jaxon trap now sprang into action. The nearby stealthy frigate, the *Pollux*, powered up and closed to attack the *Destiny*.

Hale reported, "Captain, a Jaxon frigate is fast approaching our position. They'll be within firing range in a matter of minutes. I can't move closer, or send reinforcements. They'll pick off our shuttle before it could reach you. Hold on until I can defeat this ship."

As the *Destiny* sparred with the frigate, Hawkins and his men fought a long violent firefight on the Q-ship. But their ammunition was running as low as their options.

After nearly half an hour, the Special Forces commander ordered his men to cease fire. It was clear that the rebels were close to breaking.

He yelled, "Rebels, you are completely surrounded and outgunned. You're doomed. I'm giving you ten minutes to surrender, or we'll finish the job."

Hawkins gazed at the faces around him.

I can't work miracles.

"I knew that one day your reckless actions would be the death of me," said Williams, overwrought.

Another man said, "It wasn't the Captain's fault."

Williams continued his truculent denouncement. "Wasn't it? Whose fault was it then? We didn't take a careful look before we leaped. We rushed in unprepared, as always, based upon wishful thinking."

Hawkins said, "This isn't the time for recriminations. We have to find a remedy."

"How? What do we do now?" asked one man.

"There's only one way," said Williams.

They all looked at Williams, trying to divine what he meant, for none of them could think of even one way out of the situation.

Williams said, "The only way out is to surrender."

One man shouted, "I'm sick and tired of your endless cynicism, your perpetual whining, and pessimism, and . . . and . . . if you wanted things to be easy, you should've quit long ago."

"Bah! I wish I had," screamed William.

Hawkins said, "Enough! Surrender is not an option."

He stood in the center of the men and turned around slowly to fix his gaze on every man's face, in turn.

He said, "If we surrender, this ship will join the Jaxon frigate in its attack on *Destiny* and destroy, or capture her. As long as we can keep fighting, we can forestall that calamity."

Williams said, "But we've no choice. We'll be massacred."

"Stop!" exclaimed Hawkins, angrily.

Williams shouted back petulantly, "We're pinned in this compartment, Mitchel is pinned in engineering. The enemy has superior numbers, armor, and weapons. We've only our handguns and we're nearly out of ammo. What'll we to do when we run out, rush them with bare hands?"

Hawkins turned to the short squat man, his face boiling over with outrage, "Williams if you've a mind to surrender, you have my permission to go to the compartment hatch with a white flag and surrender yourself. I'm sure the Jaxon soldiers will give you safe conduct to their prison cell." Then he scolded, "And the Devil take you—and anyone else who's of a like mind."

There was silence.

Hawkins fixed a frigid stare on Williams and said, "I, however, shall not be joining you."

Williams cast his eyes down—shame faced—unwilling to glance at the men around him. Everyone stepped away from him and he found himself alone in the center of the compartment. Sounding contrite, he mumbled, "No, sir, not me. I'll not dessert my friends and comrades."

"Very well, then," said Hawkins with a renewed flourish. "I want every one of you bilge rats, to find a deep hole or whatever cover you can, because I'm going to bring this place down around your ears."

Bewilderment crossed their faces as they scurried to find cover.

Hawkins contacted the *Destiny* and said, "Hale, we're desperate and nearly out of ammo. We're about to be overrun. There's only one chance left. I order the *Destiny* to blast this ship with everything she has."

Those around Hawkins took a moment to comprehend the order. Hawkins desperate plan was an uncompromising one. They squeezed down into any hidey holes, they could find.

Hale took several seconds before he fully appreciated the order. He asked, "Will you repeat the order, Captain?"

Hawkins repeated the incredible order.

Hale said, "Aye aye, sir."

Hawkins called Mitchel and told him what was coming.

The Special Forces commander yelled, "Time's up. Surrender or die."

Hawkins called Hale and said, "They want our answer."

Hale didn't respond.

What could he say?

Then the holocaust descended.

The Q-ship was hit with two powerful broadsides from the *Destiny* that tore through the ship. The unprepared Special Forces men were cut to pieces by the devastating energy blasts piercing the hull in dozens of places—renting, burning, blasting, and gashing the insides of the ship from stem to stern.

The compartment Hawkins and his men were confined in actually helped protect them from the worst effects of the blasts. Nevertheless, some of Hawkins' own men were among the wounded.

Williams stood up after the second broadside. He managed to shake off the debris covering his body and muttered, "That was a harebrained scheme."

Another man asked, "Did it work?"

Hawkins said, "Let's make our way to the armory and find out."

The remainder of the Special Forces men hurried, scurried, and shouted, as they tried to regroup, but after the barrage, Hawkins led his men to the ships armory and rearmed themselves.

The Special Forces men never regained the initiative. They never realized what shape they were in until they were forced to surrender to Hawkins, in ones and twos, and became his prisoners.

While the *Destiny* continued its duel with the frigate, Hawkins turned the tide on the Q-ship and gained control. He organized his men to take control of engineering and the ship's weapon systems. From the bridge he directed the Q-ship closer to the Jaxon frigate. He pretended to be the Special Forces commander and sent the frigate a message saying he was coming to help them attack the *Destiny*.

At the critical moment, both the *Destiny* and the Q-ship turned together and delivered devastating broadsides into the *Pollux*.

The *Pollux* engines were damaged and any chance of escaping was gone. She put up a strong defense, but it was clear she was now outgunned and outmaneuvered. The enemy frigate surrendered in less than hour and Hawkins led his second boarding party of the day to take possession of the frigate.

Though his pride was wounded after falling into the trap, Hawkins felt vindicated when he renamed the converted eight-gun Q-ship, the *Liberty,* and together with the frigate, named *Pollux,* he added them to the tiny, but now expanding, rebel navy.

18

A RECKLESS GAMBLE

The eight men seated at the wardroom table wore distressed nervous faces with tense furrowed brows, dark pensive eyes, and twisted pursed lips. They held their breath. Hawkins was at the head and all eyes were on him—each face prickled to see his next move—everyone waited in tingling anticipation for what they thought was the only possibility to save him from certain loss.

Hale was on his right, Gunny to his left, and Joshua sat at the other end. Every officer had his poker face on—because this was Saturday night, and Saturday night was 'poker night' aboard the *Destiny*.

Located aft of the officers' quarters, the wardroom was designed to accommodate the majority of the ship's officers in one sitting. It was where the officers took their meals, relaxed, and socialized. The computerized food dispenser provided the scheduled meals from the fresh and synthetic food stocks. There were centuries-old traditions and many unwritten rules associated with wardrooms aboard naval ships, but on this rebel vessel, things were a bit unusual and perhaps more than a bit unorthodox.

With all due deliberation, Hawkins took a sip of hot stim-coffee. He inserted a voucher into the food dispenser and punched in an order for a few snacks. Of course, these weren't real snacks, merely some synthetics with artificial flavoring, but needs must. He offered the snacks to those around him and several joined him in munching and chewing, all the while eyeing the chips in the center of the table.

The ante pot was filled with chips—and these chips possessed real value to every person there, because they represented food vouchers—vouchers that could be used for the small stash of real food available on the *Destiny*. Without a voucher, a person was stuck eating the ill tasting synthetic nutrient bars.

So the stakes were high by spacemen's standards.

"What are you going to do, Jamie?" prodded Hale who had a considerable number of his chips already pushed into the pot. He fingered his remaining chips, shuffling and rippling them, absentmindedly.

Hawkins gazed at his opponent confidently, in no hurry. He took another long sip, appearing disinterested. Then, he reexamined his hole cards, as if he had no idea what they were.

He enjoyed the occasional opportunities to interact with his officers outside of their professional duties. He found that playing games revealed a great deal about their personality—who was daring—who was timid—who learned from their mistakes.

On Saturday night, they played dealer's choice which included five-card stud, seven-card stud, and No limit Hold'em.

This hand was No limit Hold'em and there were a lot of chips in the pot.

As card games went, Hold 'em was in a class by itself. It was a complex game that required a lot of guessing—and a lot of guts. While everyone might get lucky at some point, in Hold 'em, it took more than luck to be a consistent winner. It required special skills and an aggressive gambling nature.

To Hawkins' mind, poker was more about the people, than the cards they held. It was often about making the right bet, at the right moment, against any particular opponent.

The question is; Am I right about Hale?

For bluffs one needed guts, a good read on his opponent, and a stone face. While some played tight, others played for fun, and some played to win the approval of others. However, everyone wanted to win more vouchers.

Hawkins was good at putting the heat on his opponents by forcing them to make tough decisions. He typically raised with any kind of decent hand, or any kind of draw, knowing that his opponent might try to bluff and he might catch them out.

In this hand, Hall was his only remaining opponent. Hale's hidden hole cards were Ace-King, while Hawkins hidden cards were Six-Seven, both Spades.

The flop was three cards face up; Four-Five-Ace.

Everyone was still waiting for Hawkins' play.

He made a large bet.

Hale re-raised, confident with his paired Ace.

Hawkins considered the pot odds.

There's a good chance Hale will fold, but even if he calls, I can still draw to a straight.

Hawkins went all in, pushing his large stack of chips into the middle of the table.

He'd made the choice tough for Hale. Hale liked his aces, but he worried about the drawing possibilities to a straight. He saw that the price of poker was very expense for this hand.

Hawkins saw Hale's troubled expression.

Bluffing is as much art, as science.

Hale studied his hand, one more time, and decided there would be a better opportunity, later.

He folded his hand with a sour expression.

Hawkins laughed, "You're looking at the many ways you can lose, and so you retreat. I look at the few ways I can win, which are enough for me to attack."

There is no room for sympathy in poker.

After playing against Hawkins for a while, his opponents learned that he was an unusually aggressive player. It enabled him to win a lot of pots, because if an opponent played back at him, they knew he might go all in, and they would have to make a tough choice, they didn't want to face. However, Hawkins always played hands that gave him an out, a possibility that if it hit, he would have the best hand. His style deceived and confused many opponents.

Gunny slouched in his seat, elbowing extra room from Mitchel on his left in order to fit into his seat. Mitchel, as always, sat straight up perpendicular, a result of his military background as a midshipman at the space academy where he learned his engineering. His uniform was actually as close to regulation as was possible, given the makeshift dress code on board.

Hawkins made a mental note to come up with some proper rebel insignia.

Gunny stuffed a handful of snacks into his enormous mouth.

The smell wafted about.

The green hanging curtain over the wardroom door was pulled back as a messenger handed Hale a report on the ship's personnel. He read the report and noticed that Joshua had fallen behind in his Midshipman qualifications.

"How are the studies?" asked Hale.

Joshua's smooth boyish face was often found reading poetry and novels, rather than tech manuals. His hopes and dreams had changed over the last year, but in his heart he kept his devotion to the rebel cause.

He shrugged uncomfortably at being the focus of attention at the table.

This was not the response the ship's executive officer desired. He tried again.

"Midshipman Morgan, how are your qualifications going?"

"Oh, um. Yes, sir. I'm making progress," he started, and then the flood of miscellaneous information deluged them. "I got a diagram for the ship's electrical system and was studying that, but then, I was called to stand watch, as Assistant Officer of the Deck, and then I got assigned to oversee the maintenance and repairs of the auxiliary water pump, and then . . ."

"Hold on. Hold on," laughed Hale, getting more than he bargained for. There was laughter around the table. "Maybe we'd better discuss this after the game."

The next hand was dealt and Hawkins looked down at Q-J. He bet heavy. Gunny and Mitchel called to stay in the pot.

The flop came; K-8-9. Gunny made a moderate bet. Mitchel called, as did Hawkins. The fourth card was 2 and all checked. The final card was 3. Gunny checked. Hawkins assumed Gunny most probably had top pair and was playing it slow. Mitchel made a big bet and Hawkins guessed that he was trying to steal the pot after a busted straight draw. Thinking about his opponents, Hawkins believed if he bluffed big, that Gunny would fold thinking his top pair was beat, Hawkins could then win the pot by having the best high card against Mitchel who most likely had been trying to fill a straight with J-10.

Hawkins bet big. Gunny seeing both his two opponents betting heavily, reasoned as Hawkins predicted and folded. Mitchel threw all his chips in, hoping to bluff

Hawkins out. Of course, Hawkins called and won with a Queen high.

Hawkins explained his play to his shipmates, as an example of the science of bluffing, as opposed to an empty bluff. They nodded, but he doubted if they appreciated his convoluted thinking.

Gunny tried to compensate for his loss, by smashing a large handful of snacks into his mouth.

"Got enough there Gunny?" asked Mitchel. "You must have growing pains."

The room erupted in laughter.

Gunny turned to Mitchel and teased, "I used to be an engineer, but that was before they discovered I was a grown man."

There were chuckles.

"It's always like this in the wardroom, lots of hungry mouths to feed," said Hale.

"I'm going to use my chips for something before their all gone. This'll hold me for a bit," said Gunny, as he cashed in several voucher chips in the food dispenser and built himself, a man-size sandwich with baked ham and two slices of real bread, baked fresh in the ship's galley from the basic ingredients which were also part of the booty of their last raid.

There was a lot of noise from the passage outside the wardroom where some of the crew was debating where the ship was headed.

"How's weapons training going?" asked Hale, looking at Gunny.

"Good. I can see my way to getting all weapons fully operational before the next set of target practice drills. Are you getting anxious to schedule that?"

"I already have, so if you're going to make your word good, you need to be ready within forty-eight hours."

Gunny paled, but gave a grudging, "Will do."

Hale asked, "How about the engineering repair schedule?"

Mitchel frowned, now that the attention was turned to him. He said, "I wish to report that engineering is nearly up to date on repairs and maintenance."

"Nearly? That' too bad I was going to recommend some R & R for your team, but if their still too busy . . .?"

"I wish to report that engineering has completed all essential repairs and we are ready for R & R."

Hale laughed.

The last R & R was on a small mining colony that had drinks and limited entertainment, but was nonetheless a great success. The men enjoyed staying at the cheap hotel rooms that were available, a welcome change from the crowded accommodations aboard ship. At least it included clean linen and plenty of booze.

A few hands later, Hawkins had 2S-3S. Mitchel with J-J opened, making a moderate bet. Hawkins raised a substantial amount more. Mitchel was surprise, but called.

The flop was JS-6C-7C. Mitchel almost smiled when he saw the third Jack appear and made a big raise. Hawkins thought he should fold, but he was sensing weakness in Mitchel's manner and instead decided to bluff. He called the raise. When the 8C came on the turn, Mitchel again seemed to make a nervous twitch.

Look for your opponent's 'tell.'

Hawkins decided to bluff once more, to unnerve his opponent. He went all in.

Now Mitchel was visibly concerned that Hawkins had hit a flush or a straight.

He scowled and slammed his hand into the center of the table—showing his Jacks and folding his hand.

He sputtered, "Damn!"

Hawkins raised his brows and showed his hand—a stone cold bluff.

"How could you raise against my Jacks with such nonsense?" protested Mitchel.

Hawkins sighed whimsically and said, "I've been touched by the chance, more than once."

Hale demanded skeptically, "But what happens, when you're all in, and your bluff gets called?"

Hawkins looked far away for a moment, recalling a time when he was caught bluffing as a Marine—with dreadful consequences.

His face contoured into a painful grimace.

He said quietly, "Then you lose."

19

A FAIR TRADE

Captain Jamie Hawkins was well pleased—which meant he was well pleased with himself. He sat in the command chair of his flagship surveying the column of ships that made up his diminutive fleet. He was especially proud that he had personally captured every one of the ships. The *Destiny* was in the lead as the rebel flagship, followed by the thirty-six-gun frigate *Pollux* and the eighteen-gun sloop *Retribution*, with the converted cargo ship, *Liberty*, and its eight guns bringing up the rear.

He was proud of the *Destiny's* crew, which had been with him in every action. The other ships were shaping up well, thanks to a sprinkling of his closest comrades among them. His irregular training program had brought them up to respectable standards. His delight extended to appreciation of the now several thousand rebel troops who with charged with defending the base on Spindrift.

While he readily acknowledged the multiple occasions when Fate had been kind to him, he had begun to believe in his own luck, and he counted on it whenever he embarked on hazardous expeditions.

On the other hand, he knew that actions were being taken against him—personally. Both President Victor and Chairman Rusk had denounced him by name, calling him "the greatest villain of all time" and setting a price on his head. Special operations forces had standing orders to find and eliminate him. But that attention didn't intimidate him; in fact, he considered it flattering. He trusted his men, his luck, and his own ability to pay back those unprincipled scoundrels for the suffering they had visited upon him over the years.

The *Destiny* and its ragged fleet hovered on the outer edge of the asteroid belt. For several hours they had held at maximum radar range, dodging behind asteroids to observe three Hellion warships that were attacking a Jaxon convoy with two small escort ships. The convoy of two freighters, carrying valuable mineral ore, maintained course toward the inner system while the two escorts struggled to keep the aggressors at bay.

They were failing.

"What are you waiting for?" asked Hale.

"Patience, my friend, patience," said Hawkins. "The Jaxon ships have already slackened their fire. Soon they will be helpless. There is more to be gained by delay, than impetuous action. In the meantime, maintain minimum emission standards and see how close we can get before we're detected."

"Do you expect Jaxon reinforcements to arrive?"

"Certainly not, Jaxon is spread too thin and under-manned in this area already. This inadequate escort is proof enough of that."

"Then the outcome is settled and we gain nothing by lingering in the vicinity. We should leave before we're discovered."

"Is that, what you would do?"

Hale looked perplexed, then worried. "Surely, you're not contemplating engaging in this melee in some way?"

"What I'm thinking is that the longer this battle drags on the worse off all the combatants will be. If we step in when the time is right, we may find better odds for gaining some profit."

"Hawkins, you're taking a huge gamble here. Before long the Hellion frigates will destroy the escort vessels, and even after a battle they will still be too formidable for us to tackle."

"I won't take the risk, if time proves you correct; however, if an opportunity presents itself . . ."

Hale blanched and the creases in his forehead deepened. He had learned to trust Hawkins's instincts and ability, but still, this seemed like a dangerous game.

An hour later, Hawkins sounded battle stations and ordered his ships ahead full speed toward the action. The *Destiny* came to life and bore down on the convoy. The two escort ships were now little more than wrecks, trailing vapor, smoke, and debris and maintaining only token resistance. One of the Hellion ships was also crippled and had dropped out of the battle, lagging far behind, with the second maneuvering erratically as she struggled with a direct hit to navigation. The remaining Hellion warship the *Indefatigable*, the largest and most powerful of the three, drove in to finish off the Jaxon escorts and claim her prize.

Hawkins opened a communication channel and signaled in Hellion code to alert the Hellion ships that a 'friend' approached. Once the *Destiny* Friend-Or-Foe ID was verified she was ignored by the Hellion ships and within half an hour she had closed on the remaining forty-four gun Hellion frigate.

Hawkins sent his little fleet to attack the convoy and the damaged Hellion ships while he left the 36-gun *Destiny* to tangle with the largest Hellion frigate, the 44-gun *Indefatigable*, alone.

The first moment that the *Indefatigable* knew it had been tricked, was when Hawkins ordered a point blank broadside.

Hawkins ordered, "Fire."

The *Destiny's* primary armament was a starboard broadside of half of its thirty-six dark energy laser guns.

Hawkins said, "Our enemy should be rethinking their situation—right about now."

The volcano of destruction that burst upon the *Indefatigable* was a murderous scythe through its hull.

The *Destiny* held course and kept up a withering fire until the *Indefatigable* finally turned its weapons on the *Destiny*.

Hale said, "Captain, the enemy is shifting their position. They're firing at us instead of finishing off the Jaxon escorts."

While the *Indefatigable* maneuvered to open the range, the *Destiny* turned to strike her across her stern, again hitting with good effect.

A minute later, the sensor operator reported, "Captain the enemy is changing course."

"Enemy is now on an intercept course toward the *Destiny*, Captain."

"Evasive action! Fire!"

The *Indefatigable's* first punch—missed wide to starboard.

Gunny fired repeatedly, targeting the frigate with increasing effectiveness. Joshua's voice squeaked, "The frigate is firing again."

Hawkins ordered, "Weapons; target their engines."

The *Destiny* swung hard right, spewing laser fire while the Indefatigable tried to get a lock.

The energy blast glanced off the enemy hull, inflicting considerable radiation damage, but not seriously diminishing the ship's capabilities.

Joshua reported from CIC, "Enemy is firing missiles."

Hawkins ordered the release of counter measures including radar confusing material and decoy drones.

Again the enemy maneuvered and fired ray guns. This salvo was dead on target causing the *Destiny's* environmental control alarm to flash red.

"Sensors," said Hawkins, "Range and bearing to the target?"

"Range 2 light-seconds, bearing 100 mark3."

"Lock guns on target and fire."

"Aye, Captain."

Hawkins ordered, "Helm, correct our course to match the enemy's maneuvers."

"Aye, Captain."

The *Destiny* swung slightly to minimize its angle. By virtue of its superior accumulated speed, they closed rapidly.

He squirmed in his chair to get a better view of the screen.

The *Destiny* scored another hit on the *Indefatigable's* hull.

He barked, "Helm, hard to port" just as two explosions battered the ship in quick succession.

An energy beam exploded on the *Destiny*, rocking the ship like a child's rattle. The blast overwhelmed the shields, penetrated the hull, and shocked the inertial compensators. Deep within the *Destiny*, an internal fluid tank strained under the impact, then exploded in a blinding flash. Hawkins was flung violently from his chair and the acrid stench of smoke and ash invaded his nostrils. He coughed, his lungs screaming for air.

What happened?

Sparks sputtered from the weapons control panel and a ruptured pipe spewed hydraulic fluid onto the deck. The *Destiny* shuddered as more internal systems convulsed from the impact.

Hawkins struggled to gather his senses. Only semiconscious, he thought he heard indistinct voices calling his name, but he couldn't seem to open his eyes. He wiped blood off his face, unaware of how he had cut his head and shook it, trying to clear the buzzing in his ears.

Slowly his head cleared, and he realized that the buzzing was static from the communications intercom. The voice became louder and more insistent.

"Are you all right, Captain?" Hale prodded him. "You're covered in blood."

Hawkins staggered to his feet and looked at the carnage in his bridge, then down at himself, and said, "I don't think all of it is mine."

He felt the heat, breathed the thin air, saw the electric sparks and flashing lights, heard the clamor of alarms and the groans of the wounded and the disembodied voice repeating, "Warning: Life support out of service." The sights and sounds of the ship reflected his own pain. Still he waited, waited for the opportunity to spring a counterattack.

There were rattling, hissing, clanging alarms, and a flourish of blaring sirens making the ship sound like another world. Within the ship, minor and major crises competed for attention.

Gasping for breath, heart pounding, Hawkins staggered back to his control console and croaked, "Damage?"

Gunny reported, "Jamie, the last blast took out most of our guns."

What do you do when you're out of options?

Hawkins closed his eyes and let his mind drift for a moment.

Would the enemy captain outguess him? What new tactic was he thinking of to finish off the Destiny?

What next?

Hawkins ordered the *Destiny* to move even closer. Several pencil-thin beams streaked from the enemy, penetrating her shields and striking the armored hull.

Hawkins watched his crew work furiously to restore order and functionality to his ship. Running his eyes around the bridge crew, he was proud of their dedicated response and knew he could return his attention to his main task of fighting the enemy.

The *Indefatigable* fired another broadside.

Both ships had suffered severe damage and the pace of the battle slowed as they turned their attention to repairs.

The crew of the *Destiny* worked furiously: extinguishing fires, isolating hull ruptures and restore pressurize to the compartments, taking the injured to medical stations. Propulsion still worked, but the ship had lost its maneuverability and couldn't turn, either to attack or defend itself.

A stroke of luck!

Hawkins saw that the Indefatigable had also lost maneuverability. It was headed toward the system's star, moving away from the Destiny.

Hawkins watched his men restart systems only to see them fail again. His voice was hoarse from shouting orders over the din of ruptured equipment, burst pipes, and sparking electronics.

He felt the ship shudder again from yet another internal explosion. Punching a few buttons, he asked the medical center, "What's your status?"

He sank into his chair in shock at the response, "Overflowing with injured, sir."

Then his jaw tightened and his eyes regained their steely glint. At the thought of his ship slipping back into confusion and destruction, his went into overdrive. His next series of orders addressed the sequence of fixes needed to organize the crew and bring the ship back to life.

Repair crews reported that all fires were now under control, and engineering had restored two-thirds power, and most systems had at least minimal functionality. Hale oversaw a team to clear damaged structures from the bridge.

The ship stabilized and its course straightened as the helm regained power.

Hawkins ordered an intercept course toward the *Indefatigable*. The engines throbbed under the strain of the course change, but they made the turn smoothly and closed in.

They had suffered enough damage—now it was time to inflict some.

As soon as they were in range, Hawkins ordered, "Fire."

The *Destiny's* aim was true and the frigate shook from the hit.

"Give them another."

Again the frigate took significant damage.

The gap between the ships closed, but Hawkins knew this was no time to relax—the situation on the *Destiny* was fragile.

He drove in, bringing his guns to bear for a knockout punch—targeting the destroyer with the goal of crippling its bridge.

"Fire!"

Direct hit!

He once more concentrated all weapons' fire on her engines until the *Indefatigable* could no longer maneuver. The *Indefatigable* had lost all engine control and was adrift in space, but she kept up a wicked rate of fire.

During this time, the convoy kept on course heading in system, its two devastated escorts abandoning ship. The other Hellion ships were struggling with their own problems and unable to join the battle. The *Pollux* and *Retribution* fought the crippled Hellion frigates while the *Liberty* rounded up the two cargo ships and sent men aboard to take them over.

However, the *Destiny* and *Indefatigable* were both badly damaged and drifting close together. They engaged in slugging match with their last remaining heavy guns pounding each other to pieces. However, the *Indefatigable* was the larger ship with the stronger shield and heavier weapons and it was exacting the heavier toll on its opponent.

Destiny was losing the slugfest.

The insides of the *Destiny* had taken a terrific pounding with multiple hull ruptures streaming vital air into space. Many bulkheads were shattered, and vital systems were burning. Most grievous of all was the environmental life support which was destroyed beyond repair.

Hawkins could no longer hear the ventilation fans which constantly feed air throughout the ship. Humans are fragile and they relied on their protective shell of a ship to supply them with the environment of life. The ventilation system was an essential part of that. With the failure of ventilation it was only a matter of time before they would all either suffocate from the slow poison of carbon dioxide build up or face the inevitable depressurization due to the many hull penetrations.

The *Destiny* was now a doomed ship. Destined to become lifeless, and eventually explode, within a short time.

It stung Hawkins's heart to see the havoc his ship was enduring.

Hale said, "Jamie, we've lost. Our ship is disintegrating around us. We're doomed. We must abandon ship."

"If my ship is doomed, then I'll find one that isn't."

Over the intercom, he ordered, "Prepare shuttles with boarding parties. We are taking the *Indefatigable.*"

"There's no chance," said Hale, incredulous.

"That's where you're wrong," said Hawkins. "There's always a chance."

He maneuvered the *Destiny* as close as possible to the *Indefatigable* and concentrated all fire on her engines until she was adrift. Then the shuttles full of desperate men moved to capture the *Indefatigable.*

The resistance was stubborn and valiant, but the desperate fury of the rebels with no place to retreat to, pressed on until after a furious climatic battle on her bridge, the *Indefatigable's* last remaining officer, finally surrendered.

The labors of Hawkins's crew were not ended, just yet. The *Indefatigable* had to be made fit once more. While emergency repairs were being made, the *Pollux* and *Retribution* collected the convoy, destroyed the badly damaged Hellion frigate, and chased away the other damaged Hellion ships.

One bonus of capturing the *Indefatigable* was the intact capture of that ship's communication encryption/decoding equipment. Hawkins immediately set Joshua to work on discovering how to use it.

Hawkins lounged in his new captain's chair. He was pleased with his new, larger ship, and he liked the name, Indefatigable.

Hale said, "Jamie, never was a victory snatched from so close a defeat."

His blue eyes sparkling, Hawkins looked around at his new ship.

He grinned, "I make it a fair trade."

20

MATTERS OF TRUST

I t was strange for these two men to face each other—
eyes locked—Hawkins cautious but curious, Hale self-
assured but bemused. With impatient glances, they
waited as the other officers finished their breakfast and
left them seated at the wardroom table.

Hale leaned back in his chair and let his face slip into
an uneasy amusement. He repeated what he had said minutes earlier, "I received a message from Alyssa."

He dropped a spoonful of sweetener into his stim-coffee and stirred it, slowly and methodically, clockwise—all
the while keeping his eyes locked on Hawkins across the
table—appraising his reaction.

"That's odd," said Hawkins, thoughtfully. "Why is she
sending messages to you?" He examined his friend, colleague, and comrade from every possible angle.

Hale's smartly pressed uniform made him seem powerful, whereas Hawkins' informal civilian garb made him

appear less so. In truth, neither man was comfortable, at this moment, discussing this subject.

"She asked about you," said Hale in what seemed to be an opening gambit.

Hawkins was intrigued, but reluctant to let on just how piqued, his interest was.

"What did she say?"

In a quick harsh response, Hale said, "That's personal," as if to slam the door shut on such a disclosure. However, a moment later, as if regretting his tone, he conceded, "She mentioned some mutual friends being arrested, her worry that she might never see them again . . . and she asked after you, as I said. The rest was personal."

Hawkins guessed that he might have underestimated Hale's relationship with Alyssa. He said, "Tell me about Alyssa?"

Hale sighed, "She's a pretty woman—an attractive woman—someone I've grown close to."

"We share the same good opinion of her."

Hale went on, "Did you know that the name Alyssa is derived from the name of the flower alyssum, once thought to cure some diseases. It seems appropriate that she became a doctor." He paused, and then continued reflectively, "She's the kind of woman who always finds a way to smile; the one that you'll see walking with her head held high; the kind of woman who never gives up. I admire that about her."

She's all that and more.

"When did you first meet?"

Without hesitating Hale said, "About a year ago, when I first became involved in demonstrations and protest activities. I was on an assignment to Newport . . ."

"And she helped you?"

Hale gave a slight nod.

"Could you have completed your task without her?"

"No. I needed security access to some medical records which she provided."

"Go on."

"I told her, I was there to collect information for my university records."

"So she was unaware of your early activist involvement?"

"She didn't learn about that until much later."

"You're a good story teller," said Hawkins, thinking Hale would understand exactly what he meant.

You were trying to impress her.

Hawkins asked, "Were there any consequences from this effort?"

Hale twisted his lips and took a breath, as if his conscience bothered him. "She did get questioned by security afterward, but nothing specific happened, at that time."

"The police weren't suspicious of your actions?"

"Not then."

"Were there other times?"

"Yes."

Hawkins listened in silence, as Hale related several of his early undertakings, a few of which led him into contact with Alyssa.

"Was it all business? All activist related?"

"Was *what* all business?"

"Your relationship with Alyssa."

"I did nothing that would compromise her, or get her arrested. She helped of her own accord even after she knew I was involved with protests and dissent. She has always believed in our cause and at the time, she was brave enough to take some risks." He added softly, "I grew to care about her."

So have I.

Hale remained taciturn, the wariness returned to his face. He took it further and said, "Alyssa and I have an easygoing relationship, a close friendship. Considering the time and distance involved, it's hard to say if it's more than that now, or could be more, in the future."

Hawkins sat rigidly still.

Hale continued, "It's been months, since I last saw her—at the hospital—that night you and I were arrested."

Hawkins tilted his chin up. "How did she know how to get a message to you?"

"She didn't. She just knew that if she passed a message to the local rebels, they would pass it on. We've been in the news enough for her to want to reach out—apparently."

"What about the surveillance she's been under since her involvement at the hospital?"

"I imagine that's been difficult, but she's resourceful. She found a way."

"Did she sound happy?" Hawkins asked, hoping Hale would share more of the contents of his message.

"She sounded content," said Hale, apparently not interested in giving more than that.

That doesn't ring true.

Hawkins had a bad thought. He considered punishing Hale in some minor way, to make him suffer for the discomfort he now felt. It was a petty emotion and it quickly passed.

He wondered about Alyssa.

She's attractive, but not strikingly beautiful. Yet, she possesses a principled character and the kind of caring nature that I find appealing.

Unable to restrain himself any longer, Hawkins leaned forward and placed both his hands on the table between them, he demanded, "Arron, has she made a personal commitment to you?"

Hale's brows knitted, his eyes grew dark, and his mouth contorted into a deep scowl. He acknowledged, "We haven't made a firm commitment." He stared directly into Hawkins' eyes, and added, "but I sense we have an understanding . . ."

"Well, my friend," said Hawkins, standing up and then looking down at Hale, "In that case, it's only fair to warn you, I intend to make my feelings known to her."

Now visibly angry, Hale said, "I doubt that will do you any good."

I wonder just how much strain our friendship will stand.

Just then, a bridge messenger entered the wardroom.

"Captain, the OOD said that there is a newscast transmission being broadcasted throughout the system that he thought you should hear."

Hawkins went to the wardroom communications monitor and tuned in a Jaxon broadcast reporting breaking news.

An attractive female newscaster with a somber expression spoke with calm authority, as she said, "Chairman Rusk stunned the world today, when he stated that he was offering President Victor a limited ceasefire arrangement within the asteroid belt, to begin as soon as President Victor agreed."

An equally attractive male newscaster with a stern demeanor and deep resonant voice said, "There has been no reply from President Victor, yet. We are waiting for his administration to digest this offer, but no doubt the government will issue a statement shortly."

The woman looked directly into the camera and said, "The situation in the asteroid belt has been grim since the start of the war and it is now approaching catastrophic proportions. Throughout the asteroid belt, there are hundreds of Jaxon and Hellion colonies in desperate conditions. There are many colonies that have had no relief in years. They have been surviving within their closed environmental habitats, using the stores they had when the war broke out and relying on a brisk black market trade. In addition, some colonies have suffered from raids from Hellion ships, as well as from internal colonial dissension and civil strife. Rebel sympathies have developed in some. The Eureka mining colonies, over which the war started, are facing starvation and genocide. It is a humanitarian crisis."

The camera turned back to the man. "Chairman Rusk said that, as a humane gesture, he was offering to withdraw his Combat Fleet from the asteroid belt and bring it back to Hellion for a period of one month, and to respect a complete ceasefire within the belt while cargo ships filled with food, medicine, and environmental repair equipment traveled to any of the colonies in need. He is asking President Victor to reciprocate, by withdrawing our Combat Fleet, back to home space and respect the ceasefire."

The woman said, "The terrible slaughter on the Eureka colonies has been called a war crime by President Victor in the past, so that should weigh heavily on his decision of whether to accept the Hellion proposal."

He said, "Hellion sources have said their experts will work to allow for humanitarian access to parts of colonies caught in the crossfire and provide for the creation of demilitarized areas around those asteroids. The Chairman further offered to open talks with Victor to discuss possibilities beyond the ceasefire. He even proposed to speed up adoption of a new constitution in the Eureka colonies to facilitate their future elections."

She turned to her colleague and said, "This could be fantastic news. We have at last, some hope for an end to this war."

He returned her gaze and said, "Don't get ahead of the story."

She twisted her lips into a frown and said, "President Victor has said, in the past, that he wanted to stay out of that area. He thought it was a quagmire. He proposed setting up a refugee safe zone, early in the war, but he feared defending such a haven would require greater intervention. Of course, Victor ended up bombing anyway, without much effect. Meanwhile, hundreds of thousands of refugees flooded from the colonies back to Jaxon. His haphazard policy has left us with an unenviable task. Until now, Victor has questioned whether any deal with Hellion is possible, given the "gaps of trust" between our two states."

The male newscaster grimaced at his colleague as if to rebuke her editorializing. He sat up tall in his seat, to appear as professional as possible and said, "It seems Victor has three options: He can continue the war without regard of the hardship the colonist face. However, without intervening, that consigns colonies to the slow-drip of destructive warfare. This option has the domestic political advantage for Victor of preserving the fiction that he is concentrating on protecting the home planets. Or, Victor can try to match the Hellion by attacking Hellion's client states. This, of course, would risk an open collision with Hellion's Combat Fleet. Or Victor can throw in the towel and effectively give away the colonies to Rusk, as the lesser of many evils. Letting Hellion have the colonies it chooses in order to end the war. Such a decision would surrender an unhappy population, largely centered in marginalized colonies, and lead to an inevitable post-war crackdown."

She watched him intensely, as he spoke. When he stopped and looked over at her, she squinted at him, and then said, "I don't image President Victor will get any sleep tonight."

Hawkins watched the newscast with growing impatience. He said, "The Hellion fleet hasn't attacked the inner planets, but that fear remains ever present. There were a dozen uprisings on different mining colonies against both Jaxon and Hellion, causing great suffering, but I don't trust the leaders, of either side, to solve this complex situation."

Hale was also concerned. "A dangerous dynamic."

All of a sudden, all the connections Hawkins had been trying to form, arranged themselves perfectly in his mind. He understood. Fury rose within him and he felt an overpowering sense of anger and frustration.

Hawkins said, "Chairman Rusk's offer is a distraction, a subterfuge, a cover story designed to essentially win the war. He wants Victor to be distracted by the refugees from the colonies, so they can direct an attack of greater proportion elsewhere, maybe Jaxon itself, or perhaps against the Combat Fleet in a vulnerable position. It would take some very skilled deception to manipulate circumstance to reposition whole fleets, but it can be done. I suspect that if Victor agrees to the conditions of withdrawing both Combat Fleets from their bases in the asteroid belt, back to their respective home planets, then once our fleet is withdrawn, he will swiftly discover that the Hellion fleet stayed put and that it was sweeping through our colonies invading and capturing all the big and best prizes. Then Hellion could fortify their gains and defy Jaxon to fight into the teeth of their fleet and the new fortifications—an impossible task. The Hellion tactics have a dual purpose: to flush out civilians and guerrillas—anyone left in the asteroid would be dead meat—and to destroy the Jaxon Combat Fleet when it tries to protect the Eureka colonies. The Victor government would undoubtedly fall. Its replacement would sue for a lopsided peace on Hellion's terms."

Hale said, "Do you really think they're that Machiavellian?"

"It's always a fatal error to assume your opponent is not as least as ingenious as you are. If I can figure this out, there are competent Hellion admirals, who can too."

Hale said, "So what should we do? Let Hellion win the war, so Victor will fall?"

"No. That would be the worst possible outcome. We must work to prevent this phony ceasefire from being imposed and to stifle any chance of the Hellion fleet gaining control of the asteroid belt."

Hale suggested, "I think we're going to have to pay a long overdue visit to Jaxon and meet with the rest of the rebel leadership to accomplish that."

Hawkins smiled.

I like that idea. I like it a lot.

21

HOMECOMING

The converted freighter *Liberty* carried Hawkins to his home planet. That tiny precious ball of life hung in space with a razor thin atmosphere supporting millions of fragile human beings—all feverishly working to erect monuments to their existence—none of which were visible from orbit. Once Hawkins descended in his shuttle, he began to recognize the hallmarks of humanity snaking along the surface and rising from the ground. The roads and buildings grew in clarity as he approached the outskirts of Newport.

It wasn't easy for an enemy of the state to slip past patrol ships and guards, to land on his home planet and sneak into the capital for a clandestine meeting with the leadership of a revolution, right under President Victor's voluminous nose. However, once Hawkins was in the cramped meeting room, enclosed in the dank basement of an old dilapidated building on the outskirts of the capital, he was confronted by many faces staring at him, assessing him, deciding if they liked what they saw. Dressed in his usual pilot jacket, rawhide trousers, and knee-high boots, he sported a two-day stubble.

Out of the frying pan . . .

It was rare that there was such a gathering and it would have been devastating if this meeting were betrayed to Victor's henchmen. What a crowing he would have, but such was not the case. The rebels were bound together in a cause they believed in, and betrayal had no place here. However, the rebel cause was not going well. The dozen men and women huddled together around the large conference table, stared at Hawkins, seemingly engaged, and intrigued, some hoping that their future might change with his arrival.

Hawkins matched each face with the brief introduction he had received from Hale before they entered the room. He concentrated his attention on their leader, Catherine Parker, who sat at the head of the rickety table with her followers, gathered around her. A wife, mother, lawyer, and former senator, she dedicated her early career to liberal causes. As a senator in the early Victor administration, she dared to speak out against the collusion and electoral fraud she saw, and Victor had ousted her from office. Despite his harassment, she continued to advocate for reform until Victor banned her outright, when she went underground to avoid arrest.

Opening the meeting, she said, "The decisions we make now are critical, we will set in motion actions and events of grim consequences that cannot be undone, or realistically altered. We either embark on a rewarding path toward changing the Victor government, or waste our best chance and lose our lives, as well as our followers, on a fruitless venture."

There were murmurs of agreement and Hawkins nodded.

Parker turned to Hawkins and said, "You have achieved something vital to our cause."

"Are you referring to my ship?" asked Hawkins.

"Actually, I'm referring to your achievement of giving our people the most important ingredient in any new venture of dubious viability—hope. With hope we have a chance," said Parker with charm and grace.

"I appreciate that sentiment."

Parker said, "However, Captain Hawkins, while I have no doubt of your fighting abilities, I wonder about your ability to work with our emerging organization—your ability to work with our team."

Once again, he recalled his mother's admonishments about not playing well with others. He said respectfully, "Senator Parker, I have faults, some of them serious. But I assure you, I am committed to the righteousness of our cause and I will do my best not to disappoint your faith in me."

"I'm gratified to hear that because I have prepared these orders for you." She handed him a tablet.

As he scrolled through the detailed instructions, he tensed.

Not again.

Hawkins shifted in his chair. He leaned toward Parker and said, "Senator, this orders me to turn over my ship to your chosen captain and follow his orders."

"That's correct, but that's not to minimize your contributions. It's rather to ensure close coordination between this government in exile and the military operations in the asteroid belt. My officer will be able to closely coordinate with me and guide you."

Hawkins stood up and shook his head. "No," he said.

Tension flooded the room. "What do you mean?" asked Parker crossly, "Are you refusing my orders?"

Hawkins was unable to strip out the dismay from his voice as he said, "Senator, I stopped following orders when my Marine company was annihilated at Gambaro Ridge, more than a year ago. I lost nearly everyone I held dear that day, and in the end, I was forced to make a painful sacrifice to save those who were left." He stopped, frozen by emotional upheaval. When he recovered his composure, he added, "Since then, I swore I would never blindly follow the folly of others, nor would I ask others to face dangers that I would not face myself."

Hale rose and stood by Hawkins' side.

Hawkins said, "I came here to coordinate my military operations with the rebel activities on Jaxon. I had hoped you'd welcome that and help oppose Rusk's phony cease-fire offer. But I have no intention of placing myself, or my crew, under your direct command."

The room remained silent for several minutes. Finally, Parker folded her hands together and rested them on the table before her. She looked up at Hawkins and Hale and said, "Please be seated gentlemen. We're not here to bicker and divide. We're here to find a path together."

The two men sat down.

Parker said, "I will respect your right to retain your command . . . and your independence." She paused and gazed directly in to his eyes, and then added, "But you're politically naïve, if you think Rusk's phony cease-fire offer wasn't understood by both Victor and myself. Victor will pretend to consider the ceasefire, in order to garner public support, because the public is desperate to believe that Hellion promises could lead to peace. I will, likewise, pretend to support the ceasefire for the same reason."

As Hawkins started to protest, Parker cut him off, "Don't worry. You needn't be concerned about Victor withdrawing the Combat Fleet from the asteroids and leaving the colonies defenseless. He'll never, actually agree, to Rusk's ceasefire gambit. We just need to play along for public consumption."

Hawkins said, "I understand."

Parker smiled for the first time that day. She said, "Good. Then, we can prepare for war—a war against our existing government—a war to bring about a new nation state. Together, we must work to build a government in exile—with your help, of course."

Hale and the others murmured their approval in unison.

"I agree," said Hawkins. "But while we speak bravely together—once we leave this room—we are but a handful, scattered to the winds."

Parker said, "Then it's up to us, to find more like minds, and build what must be built. For that, we will need men, money, and ships. We need everything from the basics to feed and clothe the civilian population, to the facilities to manufacture our own weapons and train our troops. When you need everything, and start with nothing, what do you do?"

Hale said, "We have to get the backing of Jaxon businessmen and fringe organizations to support our movement. And we must organize a news service to tie everyone together. How do we bootstrap all that?"

"It's easy—we lie," laughed Hawkins. When everyone stared at him he said, "We tell the businessmen and organizations on Jaxon that we are already well-funded and growing, and that they need to jump on board now, or get left behind, and then we beg, borrow, and steal whatever we need to keep body and soul together while waiting for the influx of support. We're actually so few, that it doesn't take that much to sustain us, and we're so scattered, that Victor will have to search, far and wide, to find us. But if we put out propaganda that we're ubiquitous, then when Victor cracks down, the public will believe we are important. They may choose to accept the risk and join us."

"That's bold," said Parker.

"I believe it's time to replace Victor," said Hawkins. "But I will not take action that will place our people in peril of being overrun by Hellion. They are the worse evil."

"Hellion is a distant evil," Parker agreed, "but Victor is homegrown. We're aware of the danger they both pose."

Hale said, "It may be, that something of importance has been settled."

"Our communications are going to be strained," Parker said. "I may offer direction from time to time, but for the most part, achieving success, and carrying out military missions in the asteroids will be your burden alone."

22

ALYSSA

The summer day had been perfect. Alyssa Palmer stood on her veranda and watched the white-crested waves crashing against the boulders that lined the shoreline below her home a dozen kilometers from Newport. A light breeze blew puffy clouds across the azure sky as the sun completed its downward path. A kilometer away, a picturesque lighthouse nestled against a cliff, high above a string of hazardous shoals. And on the horizon, the hazy evening fog settled in. She had stayed outside too long in her loose white cotton blouse and navy skirt, and now mild sunburn colored her arms and legs. As the first shadows of night grew, she wanted to hold onto the day, but, wistfully, all she could do was wish for another. A strand of hair fell across her brow as she turned her back on the view and went inside.

The motion, spray, and sloshing of the sea brought back memories of her youth, the long blissful days when her parents had taken her swimming. She did not weep for the past, nor regret not making more of it. However, she felt the present day walls of her life closing in around her because of a cruel government that kept her under surveillance.

"Oh, where are you, Jamie? I've seen you in my dreams—will I ever find you again?"

"What did you say, Alyssa?"

Alyssa hadn't realized she'd spoken aloud, and a blush deepened the color in her cheeks. She threw an apologetic look at her visitor and fellow surgeon, Barbara Rush.

"Oh, nothing," she said, heaving a sigh. "I've been on the beach reading novels with happy endings, but real life rarely turns out that way."

"Speak for yourself. I have my Jeffery and I'm seeing him tonight."

Alyssa sighed, "Will I ever find *my* happy ending?"

"Why don't you work on your seascape? I think your painting is lovely. It'll take your mind off of your worries."

"I find it hard to concentrate on painting anymore," said Alyssa.

Barbara laughed, one of those knowing laughs that said, "Who are you kidding? You're crazy about painting."

It seemed they had this conversation every few days when they had a break from the hospital and were suffering the lonely isolation imposed by their strict curfew.

Alyssa let out another sigh at the memory of how comfortable and mundane her life had once been, when art was her most passionate topic of conversation. Still, it was a welcome distraction from the hardship she endured now, with so many sick and injured to care for during this time of war and suspicion.

She stood in the living room looking at her art. She said, "I mean I still love painting and sculpture and music. It's just…all of that seems like something from a different time. Videos and books just don't do them justice. Perhaps if I could visit museums and go to concerts again, the passion would come back, but when will that ever happen?"

Barbara picked up several miscellaneous items scattered on the furniture and put them in their appropriate places. She said, "So why do you keep displaying pieces that you enjoyed long ago?"

"Do I? I suppose it's a distraction from work. And speaking of which, our shift starts in an hour. We should get ready."

Alyssa walked to the bathroom and began scrubbing the sand and gunk off her body. Feeling like a slob, she said, "Barbara I'm going to grab a quick shower before I go. Would you mind finishing cleaning up by yourself?"

"No problem."

Alyssa took off her outer garments and tossed them into the hamper. Then she stripped off her undergarments and threw them in, as well. Stepping into the shower, she let the hot soapy water sooth her body. She watched, mesmerized, as the water swirled at her feet and circled the drain. Several minutes passed before she realized she needed to hurry. Stepping out of the shower, she grabbed a towel. As she dried off, she felt the warmth of the steamy air swirl around her.

She cracked open the small bathroom window to let some fresh air in and listened to evening sounds of the neighborhood; a dog barking, a car pulling into a driveway, a small child returning home from play. She thought she heard a noise from the other room and called, "Barbara, are you ready? I'll be out in a minute."

There was no answer.

She dressed and called once more, "Barbara?"

Still no response. She went into the living room and saw that Barbara hadn't done much straightening up. In fact, she thought curiously enough, the room was even messier than before. Maybe Barbara had remembered something and already left for work. She groaned at the thought of driving into Newport alone.

She gathered up her personal items while still brushing her damp hair. She took a moment for a quick look in a mirror and ran her fingers through her hair one more time.

Oh, why do I bother? No one will notice anyway.

As her hand reached to open the door to the garage, she heard a noise from the front entrance. The security lock clicked and the light flashed green to indicate it was open.

"Barbara?" she called. "Is that you? Did you forget something?"

She took a few steps toward the front entrance then hesitated. The security light still flashed green, but the door didn't swing open.

"Barbara?"

She stood uncertainly for a moment, wondering. Before she could decide what to do, she heard another click. The security light blinked and stayed a steady red. It was locked.

That's odd.

She walked quickly over to look through the peephole, but the night was already dark and she couldn't see anyone. Jiggling the latch to make sure it was closed and secure; she turned back toward the side door, but stopped in her tracks when she heard a ratcheting sound coming from that direction.

Why would Barbara go around to the side of the house?

Her patience wearing thin, she strode over and yanked the side door open. The hallway was empty, no one was in the garage and Barbara's car was gone.

So she did leave.

As she closed the door, out of the corner of her eye, she caught a glimpse of someone moving outside.

Now she was fully alert.

"Who's there?"

She took a step and then heard the back door slam.

Alyssa gasped and bolted to the kitchen. She felt the first pang of raw, cold fear—deep, primal fear, like the first great fright of a child when everything was strange and terrifying, and there is no shelter, or protector, and flight was the only answer, yet her feet were frozen intractably in place.

Grabbing a large carving knife from the utensil drawer, she clenched it in her trembling fist, out in front of her. Her mouth was dry. She licked her lips fighting down terror. One slow, cautious step after another, she crept toward the house alarm by the front door. As she reached out to press it, someone grabbed her from behind.

"Aah!"

The hand holding her was powerful, but a voice soothed, "I wouldn't harm you. You're safe. It's me."

I know that voice!

Twisting out of his grip, she stared in shock, relief, and finally amazement. Her surprise couldn't have been more pronounced, as her eyes changed, from heart pounding dreadful fright to heart pounding joyful delight.

"Jamie?"

His blue eyes twinkling, Hawkins said pleasantly—as if it was a perfectly ordinary off-handed remark, under perfectly normal circumstances—"I was visiting friends and thought I'd stop by to see you."

She had spoken to him only once, and only briefly, at Newport Hospital. Yet whenever she heard the rumors of his exploits, her heart would race and her hands would grow clammy. Never until this moment had she dared to imagine that he even remembered her.

"You gave me such a fright!" she said, her eyes wide and hands clamped over her mouth.

"Sorry for sneaking around, but I had to make sure the coast was clear before I revealed myself." He gave a mocking bow. "I humbly ask your pardon. Am I beyond forgiveness?"

She stammered, "No...no." Then she added hesitantly, "Friends? You mean rebels?"

"Yes."

"You have a price on your head."

"President Victor thinks quite highly of me."

"Everyone talks about you. You're a fool to come to Jaxon at all and a complete idiot for coming here."

"A fool I may be, but as to an idiot, that remains to be seen."

"I hope for your sake you're neither."

"As you say," he smirked.

They stood staring at each other for a long moment. Her memory proved accurate—he was as handsome as she remembered. He stood with shoulders back, head high, and a warm smile that filled her with delight.

"You haven't changed," she said, biting her lower lip. "Why didn't you at least send word you were alive and well?"

"It's not easy for a rebel on the run to send messages. And how was I to know that you even cared if I was alive?"

She blushed.

"You do care?"

"Yes," she laughed—an infectious laugh, a happy laugh.

She tried to sort out her feelings. Despite her excitement at seeing him, she wasn't sure how this day would play out.

"We have a mutual friend."

"We do? Who?"

"Arron Hale."

"Oh!" She blushed.

"He told me of the part you played last year, helping him with his underground activities."

She stood there—silent—uncertain about so many things, she couldn't speak.

Hawkins stood before her with a searching gaze. "Would you consider becoming active in our cause?"

Then quickly, as if flustered, he added, "Though I would fully understand, if you were reluctant to take the risk."

"I'm glad you asked me," She said, her chest swelled with pride, "Yes. Yes, I want to help, in any way, I can."

She wanted to contribute, but she didn't yet know the cost.

Handing her a communicator and a data tablet, he said, "These will allow you to contact the local rebel agent and pass messages to me . . . ah . . . us, when necessary."

She took the devices and held them to her chest as if they were prized treasures, feeling as if she were now part of something bigger than herself. Apprehension, distress, fear, all mingled freely with camaraderie, joy, and acceptance—she couldn't separate them as she contemplated what the future now held for her.

They sat down on the sofa and exchanged glances for a few moments before she said, "Tell me about yourself and your family. There is so much I'd like to know."

"Margret and Mathew Hawkins, were descendants of the original colonists who terraformed Jaxon. At an early age, I had resolved to follow my father's profession as a soldier, but his early death, might, in part, account for my rebellious nature. My mother worked tirelessly to get me through military college. Unfortunately, she died from illness while I was a Marine fighting the Hellion. After I was wounded and medically discharged, I moved about the countryside until I finally settled in my parent's country home just outside of Newport."

"Hmm, you didn't mention anyone special in your life."

"What are you getting at?"

"I wasn't getting at anything in particular," she said. "But perhaps love is a sore subject with you."

"No, it's just...complicated."

"Won't you tell me? Or do you now consider me an insufferable snoop?"

He hesitated for a long moment. "It's my unhappy story."

He paused again, searching for the words. "There was a young woman, once. I thought she was the one, special, but she found someone else. Someone not as reckless, not as puzzling, and I guess . . . not as complicated."

Alyssa looked at him thoughtfully. "You have a great deal to learn about romance."

"Doesn't everyone?"

"How intriguing," she said.

"Intriguing?"

"Yes. We've chanced upon an interesting topic."

"Oh?"

He's so fascinating; I can't wait to hear what he'll say next.

They spent a pleasant hour, just talking—discovering each other. She thought there was a softness about him that didn't appear in the news reports of his exploits. While he told her of his adventures, she told him of her work.

She saw his passion and drive, and it filled her with awe. Everything about him was larger than life. One rapturous moment, she sat listening to his absurd stories, ready to launch into a howling laugh the moment he took a breath, and then she was equally embarrassed by his personal tales.

She found him appealing, both physically and emotionally. Despite his brutal profession, she found him full of charm and grace, intelligence and gentleness, possessing all the qualities she considered fine and noble. He was exciting and daring and fighting for things she believed in. It was exhilarating and at the same time a little frightening; he expressed sentiments that she admired, yet was capable of violence. She was not prepared for the effect he had on her.

At the moment she thought this, he said, "It's nice to know I have a confidant." He paused before adding, "Someone special."

"Yes, I feel it too," she said, blushing just a little.

"And more," he said, his eyes searching hers.

"Why," she asked innocently, "whatever do you mean?" and pursed her full, soft lips.

Her pose made him laugh out loud, and he reached over to touch her hand.

She leaned forward to meet him, her lips moist and parted. She brushed her lips against his, and his arms wrapped around her shoulders and kissed her fully. She felt herself responding to his touch.

But the promise of the day melted away all too soon.

He said, "I can see from your face, there's more to say."

"Yes," she said, but then remained quiet.

"But not now?" asked Hawkins.

"No. Not now."

Leaning over, he kissed her gently on the lips once more, and left as quickly as he had appeared.

23

ANTHONY RODRÍGUEZ

For Anthony Rodríguez, every day brought more success. He spent his days aboard his flagship, the *Ajax*, receiving briefings about the mammoth amounts of accumulated data they were collecting. It seemed to him, that the data contained the answer he sought and he would soon bring Hawkins to justice. He hoped to use Hawkins' success against him; by looking at the times and locations of Hawkins' little victories, he was beginning to discern a pattern. Hawkins did, after all, have logistic and distance limitations. It would enable him to narrow his search area.

Rodríguez raged, "Hawkins thinks he's untouchable."

Damn Hawkins. He's intelligent and he knows it—and he's lucky and he knows it—but he's not untouchable.

Some wrathful statement was justified, but he was already thinking past that, to what his next step must be. All things considered, Rodríguez thought he would have the better of the situation, if he could anticipate Hawkins' next move and be ready.

Sloops were sent out ahead of the frigates. His stealth reconnaissance commenced full sensor sweeps, but it would take time to find rebel needles in an asteroid haystack. He deployed Special Forces. While these had not yet produced Hawkins, many more rebels had been captured and sent to Zeno. Rebel ships and bases were being eliminated faster than the rebels could replace them. Soon their whole operation would fall apart.

He set up a series of decoy ships with stealthy warships waiting nearby. The search area was now much smaller.

The net is closing—Hawkins' options are narrowing. It's only a matter of time.

24

TARIJA

The diminutive colony of Tarija, in the heart of the asteroid belt, was the 'Tortuga' of the Jaxon star system. Ghostly steel husks rose high into space—and dug deep into the bedrock—apparitions of another time. It had once been a thriving mining community, but then the rich vein of mineral ore played out. Left behind were the empty shells of buildings, habitat, and mining shafts which littered the surface. Many of the structures were connected by an intertwined complex of rusted underground tunnels. The forfeiture of prosperous employment and a flourishing environment led to the replacement of miners and their families by gangs of less desirable character. Every cutthroat, villain, brigand, and buccaneer in the system swarmed to its gates to further their ill-gotten gains through illegitimate transactions and prohibited black market deals. The governments of both Jaxon and Hellion turned a blind eye to these activities, each hoping to take advantage of the disorder. As a result, Tarija became the nexus of a thriving spy trade—attracting every subversive, infiltrator, and secret agent in the star system.

It was only natural, that Hawkins would eventually find his way to this rock.

"I don't like it," said Gunny. "It's too easy."

Hale said, "It's a honey hole."

Hawkins said, "A trap is a wonderful place to find 'cheese'."

"Bah! Don't be a fool," said Hale. "The fort's not manned and there's no governing authority, no local police. The town is teeming with street gangs and undercover agents. You shouldn't set foot in this place. It's got to be a trap," he scowled. "The cheese may be tempting, but let's be smarter than a mouse."

"If things go badly, we're too few to rescue you," said Gunny, looking at the half-dozen crewmen who had come with them in the shuttle.

Hawkins remained unfazed by their concerns. He said, "I can bargain with them."

"Bargain?"

"Yes. They're underworld criminals and gangs. They'll be afraid of us. They will welcome a chance to get half a loaf easily, rather than having to fight for the whole."

"Let me go in your stead," offered Gunny.

"They said they would only give the evidence to me personally. And frankly Gunny," Hawkins laughed, "I don't think you'd pass."

Gunny rose to his full grizzly bear height and chortled.

"I grant you, you're clever at getting out of tight spots," said Hale, shaking his head, "but I fear this escapade will end badly,"

"Wait here with the shuttle and be ready to flee back to the *Indefatigable*. I'll check things out and let you know how to proceed," said Hawkins, confidently.

Leaving his frowning shipmates behind him, Hawkins stepped along an enclosed corridor of the main habitat. Encapsulated in an elongated metal tube that was vulnerable to meteor strikes, might have unsettled someone who was not already familiar with living in space, but he didn't give it a thought. He was too preoccupied with devising tactics to deal with interplanetary desperadoes.

How should I handle them?

His mind free-associated images and words, seeking clues from his natural instincts.

There was always the danger someone might recognize him, even though he was heavily disguised. He had long floppy hair, a thick beard, and mustache, all dyed jet black. His makeup gave him a swarthy appearance and his false teeth were discolored and gnarly. One added touch was a distinctive limp. Touching his breast pocket, which contained the phony passport and other identity papers he might need if confronted, he felt confident his disguise would hold up under casual scrutiny.

As he entered the bar, he let the drowsy warmth enfold him like a blanket. With an icy cold stare, his bright blue eyes observed the chamber. The elongated oak-paneled room was filled with small tables and adorned with boot-legged military paraphernalia. The place was crowded; the air hummed with secretive chatter. A few patrons glanced his way, but most studied their drinks, ignoring him.

On this dismal evening, bustling waiters moved about serving tables.

He found a seat at the edge of the room and considered each table as a potential amalgamation of enemies. He found the world of secrets to be very different from the real world of military routine.

VAROOOM!

A ship taking off from a nearby launch pad caused some glasses to rattle on the saloon bar.

At a nearby table, six men engaged in a heated discussion over large glasses of liquor, oblivious to everything around them. The remains of their meal littered the table, and one man spit on the floor.

A waiter approached Hawkins, coughing gruffly while he wiped the tabletop. He said, "It's good to see you again, sir. It's been a while."

I don't know you.

To avoid attracting attention, Hawkins said, "I guess it has. Convoy..., you know," hoping the allusion would be enough to satisfy the man.

The waiter said "Of course. We've been busy here, too. You've a lot to catchup on."

"I imagine so."

"What'll you have?"

"Whiskey."

When the waiter returned and placed the drink before him, Hawkins found a small piece of paper under it. Chugging the drink in one gulp, he nearly choked as the bitter, potent liquid burned down his throat.

Not the good stuff.

He surreptitiously read the note. "Room 223."

He looked up and the waiter nodded with his head toward the stairwell.

Hawkins went up, prepared for anything.

He opened the door and found a man standing in front of him. For several seconds neither spoke. The man was in his fifties with well-groomed long gray hair, a thin aquiline face, and keen brown eyes that examined Hawkins in minute detail.

The waiter—now this man—knew I was coming and how I would be disguised. How many others are in on the secret?

"Hawkins?" asked the man.

"Yes."

"Your disguise is effective."

"What's your name?"

"Wyden."

"You sent word that you had information vital to the rebellion."

"Yes, but I will only give it to Jamie Hawkins. Put your thumb here," he said, holding out a fingerprint tablet scanner.

Hawkins complied, never taking his eyes off the man. The tablet went through a recognition process instantly. The older man stared intently at Hawkins as the scanner reported a match and displayed Hawkins true face and identity.

"OK," said Wyden, still cautious, but visibly more relaxed.

Hawkins was still uncertain if this was a secret information exchange or a trap set for him personally.

"All right, who are you and what information do you have?"

"Everyone here snoops and spies, using either human agents or electronic data thieves. Stealing secrets is big business. Me? I'm a shadow, a ghost; I haunt the most inner sanctums of security and discover valuable gems of information which I sell to the highest bidder, in this case, the rebels. Only I wasn't going to let this information go to just anyone. I wanted, especially, to give it to Jamie Hawkins," Wyden smirked. "Meeting you will give me certain respectability for future transactions."

"What do you have?"

"I'm not exaggerating when I say these secrets are essential to the survival of the mining colonies."

Hawkins leaned forward and furrowed his brow.

Wyden licked his lips several times. He spoke barely above a whisper, "This information will paralyze the Hellion and Jaxon intelligence agencies. They prize their secrecy. Their morale will plummet when they realize this corrosive information had leaked. It will create skepticism about other secrets and deceptions."

"How did you obtain it?"

"Not easily. Not easy at all. Several of my partners died getting this data dump. People think espionage is glamorous and exciting. It's not, let me tell you. It's a dangerous business. We had to infiltrate and wiretap the Hellion secret intelligence agency, itself."

Hawkins asked skeptically, "How did you accomplish that?"

"I used what's referred to as a 'false flag.' I used a Hellion military officer who was on my payroll to approach a disgruntled Hellion intelligence officer and make friends. He was a natural. Soon they were sharing little confidences, then little secrets, and before long, great big secrets," Wyden appeared almost gleeful. "The intelligence officer never suspected he was giving vital information to an enemy agent until it was far too late. Then he had to look the other way, or else turn himself in."

"He gave you the information directly?"

"Some, but the real payoff came when he introduced our Trojan virus into the Hellion secret intelligence computer network."

Wyden smiled from ear to ear. "We stole a treasure trove of secrets, much of which is on this memory stick."

He held a small electronic chip in his hand. Hawkins looked at it and then back at the older man.

"I procured the decryption algorithms on the black market. It cost a pretty penny I can tell you."

Hawkins waited patiently as Wyden added, "I've done all the hard work. You'll reap the rewards, once you pay up."

Hawkins said cautiously, "Secrets must be checked and sources verified, in order to be believed. And even if I believe everything you said, it's possible this information was planted by the Hellion secret service."

He knew that vague or unaccounted for data would be more disturbing and dangerous than none at all.

Wyden was indignant "This isn't going to be authenticated, by you, or anyone else, in any timely manner," he said, raising his voice. "This is hot. It's hot and needs to be acted on, immediately. Take it! Take it, now."

He thrust the memory stick into Hawkins' hand.

Reluctantly, Hawkins asked, "What exactly is on this?" as he put it into his breast pocket.

"It's what the rebellion needs most," said the man, his voice dropping mysteriously.

I can't let this man leave without getting more information.

"I need to know what's in these documents before I authorize the transfer of funds."

This gave Wyden pause. "I can see you're not used to dealing with agents," he said. "I don't have time to play around."

"Are you a rebel sympathizer?"

"No," Wyden spat in disgust. "I'm not a champion fighting for freedom."

"Then why take this risk?"

"I'm strictly mercenary and I expect to be well compensated," he said gruffly.

"Can you at least give me the gist of what's on this memory stick?"

"It includes Hellion state secrets and fleet movements that may produce panic in the colonies," said Wyden becoming agitated. He handed Hawkins tablet with sections of the documents displayed. Hawkins flipped his finger over the table to read through some of the material. It was indeed fleet movement orders for the Hellion Combat Fleet. Hawkins realized that these orders made sense when juxtaposed with Rusk's ceasefire offer.

Seeing understanding appear in Hawkins eyes, Wyden said, "Time is precious, pay me. Hurry."

Hawkins decided he had learned all he could for now. He took a small electronic chip from his breast pocket and inserted it into Wyden's computer tablet. It established a link to Tarija's black market bank. It only took a few minutes to transfer the funds electronically to Wyden's account.

Well pleased, Wyden grinned and said, "Good! Good! Now, I'll do you a good turn."

The older man leaned closer to Hawkins, and in a conspiratorial whisper said, "You should be concerned about your own hide."

"How's that?"

"They're lying in wait to ambush you—just outside the bar."

"Who is?" asked Hawkins taking a careful look at his surroundings.

"Thugs, one of the nastier gangs, they call themselves the Hellion Brotherhood. They're supporters of the EMC separatists. They found out—don't ask me how—that a rebel courier was coming and you fit the description. They claim they had a score to settle with the rebels."

Wyden could be double dipping—selling information to me—and me to others.

"How many?"

"A dozen, at least."

"Is there a way to avoid them?"

The older man hesitated for a minute, trying to gauge the profit and potential loss.

"I'll make it worth your while," enticed Hawkins.

A greedy smile spread across Wyden's face.

Hawkins transferred additional funds.

Once more satisfied, Wyden said, "Come with me."

"Where?"

"I'll earn my pay to get you out. If those thugs see me, my life is forfeit as well. Hurry."

Again, Hawkins hesitated.

Can I trust him at all?

"I can't be of further help to you, if you don't trust me."

Hawkins mentally visualized the physical layout of Tarija. It was in the shape of a giant wheel, five kilometers in diameter with eight spokes leading from the outer circle to the central hub where he was now. The hub had three stories above ground and two below. There were interconnecting corridors underground between the spokes. He knew there were members from different gangs patrolling and guarding their individual turfs throughout the complex. He mentally ran through a list of gang leaders who might be open to negotiate an arrangement with him, but he knew the Hellion Brotherhood had a wicked reputation that few would challenge.

Yielding to the pull on his jacket, Hawkins followed the older man, who led him through a corridor to a side door. He opened the hatch and the stench of stale air hit him as he peaked in. The way was clear so they went inside.

The doors that feed off the corridor led to a plaza with various bankrupt businesses and empty shops creating shadows in the limited light. Wyden knew where to step to avoid the area's surveillance system. However, farther down, the corridor opened into another plaza with bars and entertainment centers full of unsavory people. The composition of this considerable crowd appeared both strange and menacing. They were a mixture of young trendy hipsters looking for a 'good time' and those who would take advantage of the vulnerable unsuspecting drunks that arose as the night advanced.

As he trudged by, Hawkins came close to a young woman and a younger man. From the strong solid figure, jet-black hair, and oval olive face each possessed, he recognized immediately that they must be brother and sister. Two older men near this couple hovered protectively and looked threatening. Hawkins wondered if the two men were body guards or villains circling their prey.

Hawkins and Wyden stepped past.

"There," said Wyden with a relieved exhale. "The elevator on your left will get to the upper level." He gave Hawkins a slight push.

An eerie sense overtook Hawkins—he imagined foot-steps coming up behind him—but there was no one there. He looked at his companion and asked, "Are you certain this leads back to my ship?"

"Nothing is certain, but it's probable. Have faith."

"Faith? You leave much to the imagination," he replied doubtfully.

The man went to the elevator and swiped his hand over a security panel. The doors slid open and they stepped in, but instead of going up the elevator dropped. When the doors opened again, all they saw was a square compart-ment with only one door, heavily barred.

EEERRRRR!

There were now audio alarms going off.

"Damn you!" cried Wyden. "You've eyes, but you're blind as a bat. You've a head, but you're dumb as a rock."

"What do you mean?"

The man was strung tight, he raged, "Didn't you realize there was a security monitor on the elevator. Your gun set off an alarm. So instead of going up to our escape route, we went down to this restricted level where we'll be confined until thugs from one of the gangs come to interrogate us."

I might have guessed, but I didn't.

"A warning would have helped."

"Are you kidding? This is Tarija. Anyone would have known better than to carry an unshielded gun."

Hawkins looked around the holding cell. He couldn't allow the gangs to get close to him. He knew his disguise wouldn't hold up to a retina, or fingerprint, scan.

"We can't stay here," said Hawkins.

"There's no choice. We're locked in. We would need a magnesium blowtorch, or some thermite, to blast our way out."

Hawkins said nothing, but narrowed his eyes in thought.

A moment later, Wyden asked, "What are you going to do?" Though he seemed afraid to hear what his companion might propose.

You never realize how trapped you are until to attempt to break free.

Hawkins took off a boot and twisted the heel to open a false compartment with a GPS beacon, a communicator, and several other small electronic devices.

He activated the location beacon first.

At least Hale and Gunny will know where I am.

Next, he used another gadget to hack the security door. Wyden looked stunned when the lock clicked open.

"Let's go," said Hawkins, yanking the door open.

BAM!

The steel door slammed behind them, and they ran down the narrow corridor, Hawkins stopped when they came to another hallway.

"Which way?" he asked.

"How should I know?" was the immediate disgruntled response.

Hawkins scanned the corridor: doorways, elevators, and stairs to another level. Trusting his luck, he turned right, but they promptly ran into two gang members responding to the alarm. Without hesitating, Hawkins punched the first man, knocking a communicator out of his hand. The other thug tried to pull out a gun, but Wyden punched him in the jaw.

Hawkins looked down at the man Wyden had struck. He grabbed the other thug around the neck, held his gun to the man's head, and demanded, "Which way to the exit?"

The man pointed a trembling finger.

"How many goons are there?"

"None."

Hawkins hit him on the head and the thug crumpled to the floor, out cold.

He grabbed Wyden's arm even as his frightened chalk-white face tried to pull away. Hawkins pulled him in the direction the guard pointed until they reached a stairwell.

They climbed the stairs and found themselves at a locked door. Once more Hawkins used his electronic contraption to unlock it and they went through to find themselves on the main concourse of the Tarija habitat inside the central hub.

They mingled with the crowd and managed to elude relentless surveillance. Silently, without protest, Wyden did as he was told.

Hawkins felt a numbing sensation, eerie and uncanny because the situation seemed like a stalemate, for while his stalkers couldn't find him, he couldn't get to his ship.

"They're looking for me," said the old man.

"They're looking for me too."

Pointing to an exit sign, the old man said, "We're going the wrong way. From now on you're on your own." He tried to pull away, but Hawkins tightened his grip on his arm and yanked him back.

"You're staying with me. I can't risk you betraying me." *Or perhaps betraying me again?*

Hawkins gave his arm a twist and Wyden said, "I won't do it again! I swear I won't!"

Hawkins said, "For now I may need you, so I will keep you close until you become a threat to me. If you try to run, I will assume you will compromise me. I can't allow that. Do you understand?"

"Yes. Yes. But will you let me go later?"

"When I'm sure it's safe. Then you can go."

"When will that be?"

Hawkins didn't respond. He continued to pull Wyden along while scanning his surroundings for a clue that could lead them to safety.

The corridor had a lot of foot traffic passing them by.

"Halt!" shouted a man who hastened toward them.

Hawkins looked up, his stomach squeezed into a knot. He realized too late that Wyden had waved his arms at this man to attract attention. The man must have been a gang member.

"Oh! God! You're breaking my arm!" cried Wyden.

"Quiet!"

As the man came closer, Hawkins said, 'Can I help you?"

"Huh?" asked the thug in confusion.

Hawkins was now close enough to slug the man. He fell back and Hawkins hit him several more times until he lost consciousness. Wyden took the opportunity to bolt and he quickly disappeared around a bend in the corridor.

Hawkins studied his dull reflection in the metal bulkhead. He looked a filthy mess, but no one should pay him much attention.

How far can I go? Where should I go?

CRACK!

A sound behind him alerted him.

Silence.

CRACK!

Closer?

Someone was concealed in a stairwell.

He ducked down. Just in time.

A heavy-set man thrust his fist at him. They scuffled. A powerful arm shot over Hawkins' shoulder, pulling him into a hammerlock. His opponent was a professional. Hawkins tried to break the grip, but failed. His throat was briefly choked, causing dizziness.

Finally, Hawkins managed to clasp the man's fingers. He pulled until he broke several. He was free again. The man pulled out his gun and Hawkins bent the man's wrist and pulled the trigger. It was over. The man was dead.

He knew there must be dozens searching for him, trying to close the trap around him.

When he reached the next intersection in the corridors, he saw Wyden being pummeled by two thugs.

Damn!

He snuck up and waved his gun. "Release him."

They jerked around and reached for their guns. Hawkins fired. They fell.

You saved me? Why?" Wyden's bloodied and bewildered face stared up at him.

"Habit," shrugged Hawkins. "Now take off. Get out of here."

As Wyden waddled away, Hawkins was grabbed from behind by a pair of rough hands.

25

OVERLAPPING LIES

The enormous paws clutching Hawkins' shoulders belonged to Gunny

"Thank goodness, I was able to navigate to your GPS beacon, Jamie."

Even though startled, Hawkins recognized his friend in time to hold back the powerful elbow blow he was prepared to deliver.

"Gunny?!"

"This way, Jamie," said Gunny. "We've got to move fast."

Together, they fled back to the shuttle.

"You shouldn't have risked it," said Hale, once Hawkins was safely aboard the *Indefatigable*.

"Ha!" laughed Hawkins. "The trouble with you is you take life too seriously. We'll all meet the same end eventually."

"Yes, but I see no reason to rush the rendezvous."

Hawkins frowned, "I couldn't send another in my place. The nightmare truth is that Hellion's counter intelligence could have been behind all this. To believe the information, I had to see everything for myself."

$\mathcal{Q}$

"Enter," said Hawkins to the tap on his stateroom door.

Joshua came in with a woeful countenance. He sat on the chair across from Hawkins without a word. He didn't even acknowledge Hale who was already sitting near Hawkins. In one hand, Joshua had a tablet; in the other was Wyden's memory stick.

Hawkins waited patiently for his young charge to collect himself.

Finally, Joshua said, "Wyden's memory stick is a treasure trove of Hellion secrets."

Once more the boy paused unable to continue.

Hawkins said, "Tell me what you've found Joshua."

"I've been working with the CIC data techs and we've unpacked the data on the Wyden memory stick. So far we've identified two Hellion Top Secrets. The most immediate is a plan for the Hellion Combat Fleet to conduct a quick 'snatch and grab' operation to occupy the biggest Jaxon mining colonies, regardless of whether, or not, Victor accepts the ceasefire."

Hawkins said, "I've done everything I could to discourage the ceasefire talks. Catherine Parker has too. Hopefully the mutual lack of trust between the two governments will prevent that from happening. But a 'snatch and grab' operation is another problem entirely."

Hale asked, "What was the other Top Secret?"

"It had to do with the assassination attempt on Victor, several months ago, that was blamed on us. The Hellion documents show that it was their assassins that made the attempt, but they claim it was never authorized by the Hellion hierarchy. The documents show that they have begun a massive man hunter, trying to find who forged the authorization orders. They are under the impression that their entire security apparatus has been penetrated by an unknown group of secret agents. They suspect us, Tarija, Jaxon, as well entertaining the possibility of a newly formed Hellion rebel group."

"I would welcome an internal Hellion uprising," interjected Hale.

There was even some talk of Earth involvement," Joshua continued, "though they don't elaborate on how that could be possible."

Hawkins said, "This mystery is growing in complexity."

Joshua said, "That's not the only mystery."

Hawkins looked at the young man and said, "Go on."

"Captain, I told you about the deep space signal I found, and you said to leave it as an unsolved mystery."

"I did."

"Well, I haven't."

"Haven't what?"

"I haven't left it alone. I've been working to decrypt the deep space signal using our AI computer with the help of a data tech, Nathaniel McClain. We've used every minute of free time, we could spare."

Hawkins was surprised, but also impressed with Joshua's initiative.

"What does a deep space signal have to do with Hellion Top Secrets?" asked Hale.

"Everything."

"You'll have to explain that."

"Let me give you a metaphor for how I solved this puzzle, because it is a puzzle."

"Go on."

"Think of a simple portrait of a woman, say the Mona Lisa. Now consider a jigsaw puzzle of the Mona Lisa—a modest picture of a woman cut into a thousand irregularly sized pieces and spread out for someone to reassemble."

"A kid's game."

"Yes, sir."

Joshua licked his lips and took a deep breath to gather his wits before presenting his radical idea to the senior officers.

"Now let's start again with our portrait of various colors of gray, brown, black, and flesh tone that shows the image of Mona Lisa. Next, suppose that I took a black felt pen and drew a sketch of Captain Hawkins right over the portrait, only I centered it catty-corner. I could still recognize the image of the woman with its stark colors, but overlaid on that, I would also see the outline of a man in ink, in its skewed position. My brain could flip, back and forth, between the two; seeing them individually, as well as a composite. If I cut this into a thousand irregularly sized pieces and spread those pieces out. Can you image how you would go about reassembling them?"

Hale said, "I don't get where you're going with this."

"Let's say a kid looked at the thousand pieces of our puzzle and was told to assembly them into a portrait of the Mona Lisa. Once he began, he would connect pieces of vivid colors and woman's image would emerge, but he would, also, see thick black lines crossing through the woman. At first he wouldn't be able to recognize that the black lines connected in a meaningful way, but eventually, as he filled in more and more of the puzzle, he would see both the Mona Lisa image and a second, dual image, the outline of a man."

They looked at him.

"That's what happened to me," said Joshua, becoming agitated. "I've decrypted a pattern in Hellion communications, and as I was decoding some of their orders, I began to recognize an overlapping pattern."

"That's great. Why didn't you just say that?" asked Hale.

"Because the Hellion secret communication pattern, I was working on—had the overlying pattern of the deep space signal, I was interested in. When I was putting the first 'image' together, I recognized the second."

"Huh? I don't understand?"

"Neither does the Hellion security forces. They think our agents have penetrated their security apparatus and are sending false orders to their ships, but the phony orders are actually somehow a product of the deep space signals."

Hawkins and Hale sat stunned and quiet for several minutes.

Hawkins said, "Joshua you've accomplished something amazing. I want you and Nathan to work full time on the connection between the Hellion communication system and the deep space signal you've uncovered. Draw on whatever resources you need. It's a top priority. I have no idea how advanced this outside interference is, or whether it's also effecting more than Hellion, but time may be short to react to it."

"Aye, Captain. I'll do my best."

Hawkins said, "In the meantime, Hale, I want you to concentrate on the immediate threat of the Hellion Combat Fleet conducting a scorched earth policy through the asteroid belt. Find a way to relay the information to those who can use it."

Hawkins used various rebel intermediaries to relay the secrets to the Jaxon Intelligence Service and the Jaxon Combat Fleet, but he didn't know if anyone would believe him, or if they did, whether they would send help to defend the mining colonies.

26

IN HARM'S WAY

Hawkins stared at the blip on the view screen. The ship had just appeared at the edge of the sensor range and he wondered if more would follow. His flagship, the *Indefatigable,* waited at low power with minimum emissions near an asteroid just a few minutes from a large Jaxon colony on this side of the asteroid belt. The rebel fleet, including thirty-six gun frigates *Pollux* and *Castor,* eighteen-gun sloops *Retribution* and *Revenge,* and the converted cargo vessel *Liberty* of eight guns, followed her.

These ships had become a fine reassuring sight for the nearby colonists who had heard troubling news reports of Hellion fleet movements in the area. Stories reported that the entire Hellion Combat Fleet had been deployed to this sector of the asteroid belt. It appeared to be methodically capturing mining colonies, one after another, while the Jaxon Combat Fleet, under Admiral Forester, remained in

their main spaceport. It was rumored that Victor had ordered the fleet to avoid a decisive battle.

"No help will be coming from Jaxon. We're on our
own. I don't know if we can make a difference, or if we'll
just add more victims to the carnage," said Hale.

"We're not exactly naked and helpless," Hawkins reassured him. "We can help evacuate the threatened colonies
and cover their withdrawal."

"As I understand it, their greatest need is transport vessels to evacuate personnel from the most exposed colonies. That'll take at least a week. Can we delay the Hellion
for that long?"

"We'll be damn lucky if we can, but we can try. I've
rounded up several more small craft and I've sent several spy drones out scouting, to give us some advanced
warning."

Hawkins sent a comm message to the nearby mining
colony, "Prepare to evacuate."

But before evacuation preparation could be started
there was an interruption.

"There's another contact, but this one is coming from
the sunward side of the belt," reported the sensor tech.

Hawkins squinted from the glare of the sun as he tried
to spot the ship in the view port.

"Sensors are picking up more signals at extreme range,
coming from opposite directions, sir."

All eyes on the bridge turned toward Hawkins.

Hale leaned over the sensor operator's station.
"Multiple ships are heading toward this colony."

"So now we have ships, coming from each side of the asteroid belt. Exciting," said Hawkins.

"Something is wrong. Jaxon doesn't have a fleet this size, in this vicinity."

"According to the rumors, Hellion is moving a fleet to grab colonies and it appears that rumor may be right. On the other hand, the ships coming from the sunward side of the asteroid belt can only be the Jaxon Combat Fleet coming out to meet them, in direct contradiction to rumors."

They watched in tense silence until the sensor tech reported, "Captain, we have two large fleets, approaching from opposite direction."

"The sunward ships must be Jaxon's Combat Fleet under Admiral Charles Forester," said Hale, "possibly forty ships, including twenty dreadnaughts."

"Probably," nodded Hawkins.

"The ones on the far side of the belt would be the Hellion Combat Fleet under Admiral Ivan Slade, perhaps seventy ships of which half would be dreadnaughts."

"Most likely."

"And we and the colony are smack in the middle," said Hale with a frown.

"Fate couldn't have planned it any better," said Hawkins.

Old fighting techniques, learned from previous battles, resulted in great fleets of ships closing with each other and fighting in whatever arrangement they found themselves in, and often boarding enemy vessels when opportunities occurred. However, recent warship construction had developed new ships capable of forming a line of battle so that their rows of ray guns, which protruded along the sides of their ships, could fire in unison at a given target, thus combining their firepower. These dreadnaughts were now the mainstay of the space fleet and were named after Jaxon's Presidents, the largest of which was the *Victor*.

Dozens of ray guns protruded from the hull in rows along the sides of ships. Battle tactics were dominated by the tactic of firing a broadside.

For example, a dreadnaught of 74 guns would have 36 guns on each side arranged in three rows of 12 guns each with the two remaining guns in the bow. As a result, ships would have to turn to show their broadsides to the enemy before firing. The fire of the rows of guns was coordinated by AI control and when ships sailed together, such as, three columns of three ships each, they would all turn together to fire a broadside. Each ship's guns would be directed by the flagship's AI control so that all nine ships fired at specific targets with concerted fire. In effect, they fired from a WALL of gunfire. In addition, the wall of ships would overlap and interlace their Unified Quantum Field (UQF) force shields to provide mutual reinforcing protection.

The evolving tactics required ships to form several single-file lines to build a two-dimensional wall of ships then close with the opposing fleet, battering the enemy until one side finally had enough and retreated. Any maneuvers would be carried out with the ships remaining in line for mutual protection.

Usually, each column of opposing warships would maneuver to bring the greatest weight of broadside firepower to bear. Since these engagements were often won by the largest ships carrying the most powerful guns, admirals maneuvered to bring their most powerful ships, as close as possible. To keep the battle line of guns from being broken at some weak point, they kept ships of equal strength in the line. The typical dreadnaught carried 74 guns, but after several years of war, they only fought indecisive actions.

Hawkins surmised that Admiral Forester intended to defend the main colonies at the periphery of the belt. The flagship, the *Victor*, and its escort vessels crossed the sun's horizon at a great distance. There were only a few warships as large in the column.

Hawkins guessed that Admiral Slade was making a show of strength, but it didn't seem likely he would engage in a major confrontation.

As the minutes ticked by, Hawkins wondered when the fleets would discover each other. The *Indefatigable*'s bridge crew was unusually quiet in the tension.

As the distance between the fleets shrank, Hawkins ordered, "Battle stations."

CLANG! CLANG! CLANG!

Throughout the *Indefatigable*, the crew responded. Weapons were charged, but energy consumption was minimized for low priority equipment, environmental controls were adjusted with all compartment hatches battened down. The ship maintained it low emission state making it hard to detect at normal distances.

As the crew's youngest member, Joshua was eager to report to the CIC to track the enemy ships. With his thin frame and slight build, the busy crew hardly noticed him.

"All battle stations manned and ready, Captain."

"Great," said Hawkins, furrowing his brow. "Give me each fleet's course."

Seconds later, the astrogator reported, "The Hellion fleet is steering course 010, mark two, sir, heading almost directly toward the sun."

"The Jaxon fleet is steering course 190, mark 2, sir. Fleets are converging on the nearby colony."

Hawkins mind raced, seeking some additional resources that would help him sway the impending battle in the *Indefatigable's* favor.

"How long before we're in range?" asked Hawkins.

The sensor operator said, "An hour, Captain."

Hawkins watched the amplified view screen in fascination as the fleets approached.

He watched for any change to the enemy's trajectory, looking for any indication that they had discovered the approaching Jaxon fleet.

Admiral Forester of the *Victor* formed his forty ships into a double line of battle with ten dreadnaughts leading each column. His twenty lesser ships following behind the dreadnaughts at a respectful distance, intent on providing what limited support they could offer.

He had received reports that the Hellion fleet was in this area and he guessed they would assault the local mining colony. He didn't intend to let that happen.

He turned to his bridge officers and said confidently, "Victory is assured!"

His men responded with a hearty cheer.

One of Jaxon's scout drones reported the Hellion fleet at some ten light-seconds distance.

Ship time read 5:30.

The captain in the lead ship reported, five enemy ships heading toward the mining colony.

The Jaxon fleet adjusted course slightly toward the Hellion ships. They completed their maneuver and settled in their new formation and course.

The bridge was alive with crewmen scanning their instruments for more details, chattering excitedly.

"I wonder what old Forester is thinking," one muttered.

Forester had no idea of the size of the fleet, he was up against, but as the ships loomed up, a sensor lieutenant exclaimed, "Those are some real whoppers!"

On the bridge of *Victor*, the flag captain reported the count of enemy ships as they came into existence on the ship's sensors.

"There are twenty Hellion ships, sir."

"Very well."

A minute later, "There are thirty ships, sir."

"Very well."

And again moments later, "There are fifty, sir."

"Very well."

"Sir, there are now . . ."

Forester's back stiffened. "Tell me no more. No matter if there are a hundred enemy ships, I will not shirk."

Forester pulled on his right ear, a mannerism he had in his adult life, indicating he was lost in thought.

The fighting formations in space warfare, particularly in attack, were characterized by massing concentrated gun fire at the critical point of battle. The Hellion were prone to sacrifice men at an alarming rate, in order to get into an advantageous position. They displayed contempt for the lives of their men. Their ships would attack in waves. Such ruthless methods sometimes produced results, but the cost in morale to their own troops was enormous, producing a lack of enthusiasm in their lower ranks.

On the other hand, the Jaxon ships were generally in poor condition due to Victor's corruption, preventing them from taking swift advantage of these tactical situations.

Neither side was able to improve very much on the battle field, bound by strategies of rigid thinking.

The Hellion fleet was formed in three parallel divisions of twelve dreadnaughts each. Like an octopus it extended its tentacles toward its prey. Each of the divisions of dreadnaughts was a threatening appendage. The fleet had a large outer screen of sloops and frigates. The outer screen formed a quilt-like arrangement. The overall effect solidified the volume of the outer screen. The main battle fleet was about ten light-seconds ahead of a support force that included transports and supply ships which they used after capturing a colony. But the support ships were slow and ponderous, and now they were a burden for the Hellion Combat Fleet to protect them.

"What's the range to the Hellion fleet?" Hawkins asked.

"They are within firing range of the colony, sir."

Something about one of the defense satellites appeared strange. A moment later, it exploded and disappeared from the screen. Then, another bright flash appeared on the view screen. The Hellion ships were shooting at the colony defenses.

CIC reported, "That last explosion may have caused serious damage to the asteroid's surface, but we're uncertain how close it was to the populated area."

Hawkins grimaced and nodded.

The sensor operator reported, "We're still undetectable on the enemy's sensor range, sir. They wouldn't be detecting us at any time soon."

"Good," he said. "The Hellion should be sensing the Jaxon fleet by now."

"The logical question is as the Hellion maneuvered to attack the colony, will the Jaxon fleet arrive in time to help?" asked Hale.

"Once they realize the Jaxon Combat Fleet is approaching, they may change their plans," said Gunny.

"For the moment our focus should be on how we will respond," said Hawkins.

"This means anything we attempt, will be playing catchup."

"Indecision, in the face of the enemy is paralyzing, and is the cause of many defeats," said Hawkins.

"I don't like the sound of that," said Hale.

"It doesn't matter what you want, it only matters what we can accomplish," said Hawkins.

"I'd advise caution," said Hale, scratching his chin. "We can't face those dreadnaughts,"

"We may not have a choice," said Hawkins.

"Are you counting on surprise, or just blindness on the part of the enemy?" asked Hale.

"Even if we do everything right and achieve complete surprise, we'll still be badly outnumbered and outgunned, not a winning combination," said Hawkins. "We'll do well to remain hidden and sneak away when the fleets engage."

Admiral Forester asked, "How long before we're in firing range?"

"Thirty minutes, Admiral," said the flag captain. "But I must point out that we are badly outnumbered."

Admiral Forester's jaw tightened and his eyes flashed, "I am counting on the pride and courage of my men to carry the day."

The flag captain said, "I'm afraid I can't share your optimism."

"Just obey my orders and leave the optimism to me."

"The enemy is no longer accelerating toward us in a single battle line of dreadnaughts," said the flag captain. "Their ships are staggered in attack formation."

"Increase the scan rate," ordered Admiral Forester.

Why run another scan? The news will not get better.

Adrenaline made his hands tremble. He took a deep breath.

Hawkins tore his gaze from the panel to look at the sensor screen.

"That's odd," said the sensor tech.

"What is?"

"It might be a ghost sensor reading."

"Holy hell!" the sensor tech cried, blanching deathly pale.

"What the hell do they think they're doing?" asked Hawkins, looking at the chilling pale blue screen with its flashing dots of light and its pop-up data boxes describing a battle field with a frightening array of ships.

"What's the range?" he croaked.

"Two light seconds."

The sensor tech said, "But Captain, the Hellion fleet is turning around and going back the way they came. They're avoiding the engagement."

"Will the Jaxon fleet be able to catch them?"

"I'm afraid not, sir, they're too far away."

Hawkins considered his options. The wisest plan would be to stay out of sight and sensor range.

But after a moment, a strange feeling struck him, the same feeling he often got when he saw an opportunity emerge from a pattern of possibilities. He could not say exactly, what it was that triggered the idea in his mind, but now, he felt as if he were on the edge of a precipice, about to step off into a dark nothingness.

He stood up from his command chair and put his hands on his hips.

Hale, his face, a contortion of unhappy recognition and instant distress, rose to his feet without any place to go, "No, Jamie. No! Tell me you're not going to do what I know you're going to do."

"Helm, ahead full!" said Hawkins with relish. "Come to an intercept course with the lead dreadnaught in the Hellion rear guard."

"Aye, Captain."

"Gunny, full power to shields, charge all weapons."

"Aye, captain."

"Comm, signal the rebel fleet to power up and follow us."

The sudden appearance of Hawkins six ships on all of the Hellion's scan screens must have been a stunning surprise. The reaction of the Hellion rear guard was to protect its fleet withdrawal by turning toward Hawkins's ship and attacking.

"What we are about to receive . . .," said Hale shaking his head.

Hawkins intended to use his little flotilla to cut off the Hellion rear guard of six dreadnaughts from the rest of its fleet. This would force the Hellion admiral to choose to either turn back to support his cut-off ships, and thus become embroiled in a major action with the soon-to-arrive Jaxon fleet, or abandon the rear guard to fight its way past Hawkins on its own, which would mean that they would inevitably fall into action with the main Jaxon fleet, dooming them.

Regardless of the Hellion admiral's choice, Hawkins and his ships would be in the thick of battle between two opposing fleets, both of which wanted him dead.

"Don't open fire until I say. They don't know how much fire power we're packing and I want to reserve as much surprise as possible. At least until we are at our best weapon range."

"Sir, they're trying to jam our comms."

"Increase power and override."

He watched the display with calm detachment.

The rebel fleet closed with the Hellion rear division of six dreadnaughts. *Pollux* and *Castor* were closest behind *Indefatigable,* but were farther from the sun and therefore closer to the Hellion dreadnaughts. As a result, they were the first to come under fire.

Steady streams of deadly radiation blasts were released.

"Range decreasing."

"Open fire."

"A hit."

"Keep firing."

The ships charged forward.

He looked at the damage report panel and saw it light up like a pinball machine.

Two more hits on the *Indefatigable.*

Smoke billowed up on the bridge, creating a blazing pocket of hell sizzling circuit boards.

But she scored too. They ripped at one dreadnaught.

"Hard to starboard."

"Aye sir, . . ."

The combined firepower of Hawkins three frigates was enough to wound the lead dreadnaught. The injured ship limped out of formation.

Grinning from ear to ear, Hawkins ordered, "Send this message to the *Victor*:

> 'Greetings Admiral Forester,
> I have the honor to report that forces loyal to Jaxon have taken it upon themselves to aid you in your efforts to bring the Hellion fleet to battle. We have cut off and engaged the rearguard of the Hellion fleet. I suspect that Admiral Slade is making a tough decision right about now, but I think in the end, he will turn around and come back this way. While I'm sure we will give their rear division a sound drubbing, I would appreciate any assistance you might offer to deal with the rest of the Hellion fleet.
> Regards,
> Jamie Hawkins'."

Hale rolled his eyes.

They continued to fight while they waited for Forester's reply.

They didn't have to wait long.

The comm tech reported, "Message from the *Victor*, sir.

> 'Captain Hawkins,
> You do credit to your reputation.
> Good luck.
> Fleet Admiral Charles Forester'."

"Good luck? That's it?" squawked Hale in obvious distress.

"Sir, sensors show the *Victor* converging on our position," said the tech, practically cheering. "The rest of the fleet is following!"

"I hope those dreadnaughts are faster than they look," grumbled Hale.

The Hellion admiral proved of stronger mettle than many would have thought. He turned his fleet back toward Hawkins, his rearguard, and the approaching Jaxon fleet.

Hawkins had achieved his objective, but would now pay the price for his reckless decision.

As the pitched battle continued, three of the dreadnaughts converged on the *Pollux*. After several volleys the *Pollux* suddenly exploded in a spectacular, brilliant fireball.

"Oh, my God," cried Hale.

The bridge of the *Indefatigable* stood stunned.

Hawkins was dumbfounded—guilt flooded his soul. He stared mesmerized at the screen that showed a field of debris—all that remained of the *Pollux*. The pain and despair was awesome and his mask momentarily dropped away, exposing a pained expression. He closed his eyes and dropped his head in his hands. His mind reeled with the possibility that he had made a terrible mistake and done exactly what Hale had feared earlier: added more victims to the carnage.

The sense of reckless absurdity with which he had first approached this battle evaporated, replaced by deadly solemnity.

Perhaps it was already too late. In a few minutes, his rebel command would be so entwined with the Hellion ships that there would be no possibility of retreat. A deep flush rose in his cheeks. There was no more time. It was too late for second guesses, or for "if only, or maybe."

Anger drove away his fear, doubt, and anguish. His heart pounded against his ribs like a drum beat.

What is the enemy planning?

Holding his present course would expose the *Indefatigable* to a withering fire. His best plan was to fire and dodge, before counter blows were delivered. His ship handling would be critical.

"Helm," he ordered, "change course to intercept the lead dreadnaught. Ahead flank."

The *Indefatigable* came around to fire its broadside on the lead dreadnaught.

The two ships fired simultaneously.

Hawkins knew that the enemy was powerful, well drilled, and prepared for action. He was also aware that he had a slim chance in a ship-to-ship slugging match with a dreadnaught.

The dreadnaught focused all its firepower on the *Indefatigable* exclusively, ignoring the other ships.

Hawkins paced across the back of the bridge. Suppose he was drawn into close action against this ship. What were his chances? Would his shields hold or his weapons be powerful enough? The odds of a frigate against a dreadnaught ordinarily would have been inconceivable, but the *Indefatigable* had already proved she was no ordinary ship. He shook off the black mood. He had no time for introspection; he had to find some creative way to rid themselves of this attacker.

We may be outgunned and outclassed, but we won't be outfought.

They were shocked by the power of the next broadside. There were considerable casualties, including Joshua who was wounded and carried from CIC by the med tech, down to the medical center.

Hawkins reassessed the situation and revised his plan. He vowed the next broadside exchange would be different. It was becoming an exhausting struggle. He maneuvered his ship trying to shake his determined pursuer, hoping to convince them that they were chasing a ghost.

The seconds passed like minutes as the *Indefatigable* plunged further into the battle space with every crew member feeling the stress. The corridors were choked with disconnected wires and ruptured pipes extruding from the bulkhead and entwined through grates that supported the overhead deck. In was no coincident that all the circuits were out and the AI controls were limp. There were odd noises coming from all directions indicating problems and damage, but too few crewmen available to plug the holes.

Admiral Forester ordered his fleet to attack at flank speed. He knew the situation would only get worse if the Hellion fleet rejoined with its rearguard.

After several minutes, it became obvious that the Hellion dreadnaughts ships were formed in three loose columns, one of about 20 ships to sunward and another, of about 14 ships, somewhat closer to the colony. This gave the impression that they might form a single line and pass along the sunward column of the Jaxon fleet, exposing one column of the Jaxon fleet to the entire fire of the larger Hellion force.

Forester gave his order, "Form in a double line of battle behind and beside of the *Victor* as most convenient."

When this order was completed his fleet had formed a double line of battle, flying directly at the Hellion fleet.

"Engage the enemy," Forester signaled.

The two fleets met. Forester's concentration was now well and truly focused on the screen displays, as he tried to fit all the information into his brain to devise his next move.

Jaxon had the advantage, in that the Hellion fleet was split into two groups and was unprepared for close battle, while the Jaxon fleet was already in line. Forester ordered the Jaxon fleet to pass between the two groups, minimizing the fire they could launch into him, while he could fire in both directions.

After ten minutes, *Victor* tacked to reverse her course and take on one of the Hellion columns individually. The Hellion division now put about to port with the intention of breaking the Jaxon line at the point where the ships were tacking in succession. The ships came round, and gave covering fire.

As the *Victor* came to, the leading Hellion, the flagship, closed in and gave her a raking broadside.

The column accelerated. A pair of lumbering damaged ships trailed well behind. The column proceeded to the intercepting point at breakneck speed.

As the last ship in the Jaxon line passed the Hellion, the Jaxon line had formed a U shape with *Victor* in the lead. Then a Hellion division bore up to join their rearguard compatriots.

The scanner went dark and he held his breath for several seconds until it recovered. The admiral's heart pumped faster with each new data point of disappointment. There was evidence that his sensors were corrupted and offering false images.

Got to know what's happening.

Forester made a signal, "Engage the enemy more closely."

The enemy formation was in possession of the strategic advantage which could spell the doom of the Jaxon fleet if properly exploited.

"Admiral I have a damage report."

"Not now."

"Admiral I have reports of damaged and destroyed ships coming in."

"Not now, I've got to think."

The main Hellion battle force tightened its formation, but kept coming straight at the outnumbered Jaxon fleet. The movements were precise. Previous encounters had shown that the Jaxon ships had a slight technological advantage in weapons and defensive systems, but the Hellion were more maneuverable and slightly faster.

They were acting like a stalking school of sharks. In fact, they looked more like a long line with their fastest ships far in front. Clearly they intended to cripple as many ships as they could and leave them for annihilation later.

Now it was Forester's turn to unleash his power and strike back. They surged forward to meet the enemy. It wasn't going to be all one sided. Their fire ripped at the enemy brutally wounding many.

The thermal wave of destruction flickered. One ship exploded and went supernova.

At that critical juncture, Forester ordered his frigates to launch an all-out attack by charging at the Hellion ships to disrupt their formation.

✑

Hawkins led the *Indefatigable* towards the rear of the Jaxon line, much closer to the larger group. He came to the conclusion that the maneuver could not be completed. Unless the movements of the Hellion ships could be thwarted, everything so far gained would be lost. Hawkins gave orders to maneuver the ship and to engage the smaller Hellion group.

As the distance between the rebel fleet and the rearguard decreased, the Hellion fired and scored some hits, damaging nearly all the rebel warships.

For a moment, Hawkins faltered. Then he told himself, *We can do it*, casting out his troubled doubts.

The Hellion flagship, the *Rusk*, was directing its ships to attack the leading rebel units.

The rebels exchanged laser and plasma fire at close range. A frigate moved hard to port, readjusting its position to meet enemy fire. The salvos were falling on target, but they did not have enough forces to cover their flanks, so the Hellion was moving around them. There was little chance of them escaping unscathed from the ships' withering fire.

Hawkins could make out several frigates on courses directly toward the *Indefatigable*, firing, and then reversing course. After taking a hit, one frigate slowed and fell behind. It became easy prey for the following ship. The hapless ship struggled to get away, but it was marked by explosions of orange flame until the destroyer finally disappeared in a bright flash.

Hawkins directed the *Indefatigable* to cross ahead of the Hellion ships in that group which included the largest ship ever built, the *Rusk*, the flagship of the Hellion fleet.

Hawkins's decision was significant. *Indefatigable* gradually overhauled the *Rusk* and began a close engagement. Momentarily the *Indefatigable* was under fire from as many as three Hellion ships. Soon however, several Jaxon dreadnaughts caught up with the *Indefatigable* and supported her fire.

Moments later, three Jaxon dreadnaughts commenced an attack on the *Rusk*, with one stationing herself on the bow and another on the quarter of the Hellion ship. Observing that the *Victor* was about to pass close astern, the *Rusk* judiciously hauled down away and called for assistance from her fleet.

Victor's guns came to bear with effect.

It was almost twenty minutes later that *Indefatigable* was in close action with another Hellion ship. By now her guts were shot out, but she continued to fight.

In a few more minutes, Hawkins ordered his severely damaged ship on a course to escape the action.

Both Hellion vessels, he had engaged were successfully captured by Jaxon ships, moments later. A Hellion dreadnaught exploded.

By the time *Rusk* had also surrendered, an entire group of Hellion dreadnaughts were so damaged that they too surrendered. After the *Rusk* was captured, the confusion amongst the Hellion fleet was so great that they were unable to use their guns without causing more damage to their own ships than to the Jaxon. The Hellion men fought fiercely without discipline.

About half of the Hellion fleet fled the battle area, leaving their damaged brothers to surrender to the Jaxon fleet.

Admiral Forester signaled his fleet to recover his damaged and disabled vessels while his frigates were directed to take the prizes in tow. The fleet was ordered to take station in line astern of *Victor*.

It was a great victory for the Jaxon space fleet—40 Jaxon ships had defeated a Hellion fleet of 70, and the Hellion ships had a greater number of guns and men. But, Admiral Forester had trained a highly disciplined force and this was pitted against a demoralized Hellion navy under Slade.

"Admiral Forester! The rebel ships are withdrawing from the battle area, sir," reported the sensor tech.

"Humph," was the Admirals only reply

His chief of staff asked, "They're badly damaged—some of them crippled. A small task force could easily finish them off, sir."

"Humph."

"Sir, they're out of weapons range now! We'll lose them from our scanners in a few minutes."

"Humph."

The remaining rebel ships receded into the distance with impressive speed. Soon they were no more than a few spots of light on Admiral Forester's monitor.

A moment later they were gone.

27

THE BAD SEED

After several weeks resting in orbit over Spindrift, the *Indefatigable* was recovering from her severe wounds and Hawkins was enjoying a rejuvenating sleep. When somewhere far away, above the background hum that disturbed the otherwise silent room, he heard the faint ghostly murmur of voices, and then, after a moment there was nothing but silence once more. He thought the darkness had hushed the secret whispers until a soft knock rapped on his stateroom door.

He muttered, "Enter."

He thought he heard a muffled, "I'm first."

Then a bridge messenger entered.

"Captain, we've received a message."

"Let the OOD handle it," said Hawkins, turning over and pulling the covers over his head.

"He sent it to you, sir," said the messenger, biting his lower lip, and shifting his weight from foot to foot.

Throwing the covers off, Hawkins swung his legs over the side of the bunk and let his bare feet touch the cold metal deck. It was with a lazy temperament that he faced the day and he waited for a moment before taking the tablet. He stared at the screen with uncomprehending eyes for several seconds before he said, "Lights."

The illumination materialized the letters, but he was slow to comprehend the import of the words.

> Captain Hawkins,
> I'm willing to honor the prison exchange arrangements you offered several months ago. I'm sending a transport to Tarija with four hundred rebels in exchange for a like number of Jaxon soldiers.
> It's my hope that before long further rapprochement will be possible.
> Admiral Forrester
> Commander Jaxon Combat Fleet

Hawkins ordered, "Ask Mr. Hale to come here."

"Aye aye, sir."

A few minutes later, Hale read the note and commented, "This is a good sign."

Hawkins nodded.

Hale added, "Perhaps, we've fostered sympathy from some in the Jaxon Navy."

"Perhaps."

"In addition to the prisoners, we should send our wounded to Tarija. They'll get better medical treatment there than we can offer here."

"I agree," said Hawkins, then after a pause, he added. "Include Joshua. He's on the mend, but it would do him good."

"I'll make the arrangements."

Before Hawkins could shoo Hale away, another tap was heard.

"Enter."

"Can I have a few minutes, Captain, seeing as how you're already up?" said young data tech Nathan McClain.

This must be another of the secret whispers I heard this morning.

"OK, Nathan, what can I do for you?"

Hale made room for the young man.

"I was working on the deep space signal with Joshua until he was wounded. Since then I've been on my own, and today I found . . ."

Nathan threw his hands in the air excitedly.

Hawkins said, "Calm down, Nathan. Start at the beginning and tell us the whole story." He leaned back on his bunk to get comfortable because he suspected this was going to be some tale.

Nathan brightened and said, "You're going to love this. Huh . . ., sorry, sir, I mean . . ."

Hawkins smiled, "Never mind. Go ahead."

"I followed Joshua's example and decoded the encrypted Hellion secret orders while at the same time examining the overlaying deep space signal. I found that the signal contained an embedded digital code. Several years ago, when Hellion cybersecurity started collecting the signal pulses for examination, the embedded virus infected their network and created an alien program."

Nathan paused to take a deep breath and waited for his senior officers to digest the information.

"That's quite a leap," said Hale.

"It's all I could make out from the puzzle I've been working on, sir."

Hawkins said, "Did you verify that there aren't any human colonies in the vicinity of the signal's origin?"

"I checked. There aren't. The signal can only be of alien origin. And the nearest possible source is 44.4 light years away. If that's not the origin, then the signal could be very ancient and might have traveled through space for eons."

Hale turned to Hawkins and said, "It could be an ancient alien weapon unleashed at a long dead enemy."

Hawkins said, "Or a weapon of mass extinction."

Nathan licked his lips and said, "But that's not the best part, sir. I've found out *who* is sending the fake orders."

"Spit it out man," said Hale impatiently.

"Captain Hawkins!" said Nathan.

The three remained silent for a full minute before Hawkins asked, "How does my name figure in this puzzle?"

"The alien program created phony orders for the Hellion security force to assassinate President Victor and left evidence that 'Captain Hawkins' was the culprit behind the orders."

Hale said, "Much too clever for a prepackaged program. It not only threatens Hellion's primary enemy, but simultaneously casts blame on another rival."

Hawkins said, "We're dealing with an alien artificial intelligence."

"Yes, sir, that my conclusion too. The initial signal must have been a simple replicating virus that evolved into an AI."

"And now it's working out how to further its own survival within our world," concluded Hale.

"Good job, Nathan. Continue to work on this. It's a major priority."

"Yes, sir," said Nathan.

After the young man left, Hale said, "I guess it's my turn now."

Hawkins sighed.

Hale said, "Alyssa sent a message."

"She sent a message to you?"

"No. She sent a message for you."

Hale abruptly left—leaving the message on Hawkins' tablet.

Hawkins considered Hale his close friend, and it suddenly occurred to him in a strange and bitter way, that their friendship was under threat from another whom he hoped would become his closest friend—Alyssa.

28

AN UNWITTING CHOICE

Rodríguez sat motionless in the Special Forces Data and Intelligence Analysis Center glaring at his maps. It was unlikely that there was more to be gained from decoy traps. The rebels had become too wily. Hawkins had gotten into his head, somehow, and the frustration was exasperating.

What if I could reverse that?

A realization materialized in his mind, and with it, a sense of purpose appeared.

I can reverse that!

With great deliberation, Rodríguez said, "I may have a solution to the Hawkins Problem."

"That would be a relief," said Admiral Samuels, turning away from the digital display monitor and focusing his attention on his commander.

"As with all breakthroughs, the answer is obvious in retrospect."

"Oh?" asked Samuels, eagerly.

"Until now we've searched vast stretches of space, placing traps in likely locations, all to no available. We've been trying to go to him. What we need to do is make him come to us," said Rodríguez.

Samuels appeared puzzled.

Rodríguez said, "I've been studying Hawkins's behavior. I've come to understand him. I know how he thinks, how he reacts to opportunity, and most importantly, how he reacts to threats."

He curled his lips into a twisted smile, relishing the moment. "Everyone needs a purpose in life—a meaning to make them feel fulfilled. I've come to realize that catching Hawkins comes down to motivation."

He looked directly into Samuels' eyes and asked, "What motives Hawkins?"

"He's a revolutionary. He wants to change the government."

"No, he actually came to that cause, very late. That's not his primary motivation."

"Money?"

"No, his 'Robin Hood' complex is unmistakable."

"Power?"

"No, again. He commands, but does not rule."

"What then?"

"People," said Rodríguez. "The welfare of others. He's driven by the *need* to protect those he cares about—the people for whom he is willing to make great sacrifices."

"The rebels? The colonists?"

"Yes, to some extent, but more specifically, a select few. In particular, a young woman named Alyssa Palmer who I've had under observation for some time. She may be the opportunity we've been looking for."

"How does this help us capture Hawkins?"

"Isn't it obvious? We imprison as many of these individuals as possible in Zeno. Hawkins will attempt to rescue them."

"He would realize it was a trap and know that any rescue attempt would be foolish."

"Not just foolish—utterly reckless," said Rodríguez. With a faraway look in his eyes, he repeated, "Utterly reckless."

Rodríguez knew he was right. He knew with absolute certainty that Hawkins would take great risks under the right circumstance. He knew that with the right motivation Hawkins would come to Zeno regardless of the danger. With this knowledge, he could reasonably predict Hawkins's rescue plan and plot appropriate countermeasures. Even if Hawkins did escape his trap the first time he would keep coming back until he either freed the prisoners or died trying.

More than anything, Rodriguez yearned to be proven right. Soon everyone would know that he was right. And he *was* right, of course. Any other contemplation was impossible.

Rodríguez proclaimed that in honor of the rebel's contribution to the recent Combat Fleet victory, any rebel who turned himself into the Jaxon authorities would receive amnesty. He knew Hawkins would never accept amnesty, but under this ruse Rodríguez rounded up colonists and citizens, detained them for "processing."

He had Alyssa Palmer arrested on trumped up charges to include her in his collection.

He was particularly pleased when he discovered that one of his routine roundups picked up Joshua Morgan from a colony hospital.

The new prisoners were swiftly shipped off to Zeno and placed under Seward's watch.

As was becoming a habit, Rodríguez was having an acrimonious discussion with his deputy.

"Amnesty is meant to be a pardon, a reprieve, and chance to start life over again," said Samuel.

"I'm . . ., I'm giving them a chance—a simple opportunity to redeem themselves by playing an unwitting part in helping to catch Hawkins."

"Your use of this ruse is a cruel deception," said Samuels.

Rodríguez said, "These disloyal mining colonists are a scar on the face of our star system."

"They're our people."

"They're irresponsible stupid poor fools living on airless frozen rocks constantly begging for the scarce resources of Jaxon."

THUMP!

Admiral Samuels pounded the table.

With sternly disapproving eyes, he protested, "It's dishonorable to not fulfill our amnesty commitment."

If Rodríguez was surprised, he didn't show it. His hard eyes flashed and he said in a husky voice, "Let me worry about your guilty conscience."

What followed was an intemperate series of blasphemous obscene invectives that spewed from Samuels's mouth.

Rodríguez barked, "Hold your tongue!"

He stood up and pushed back his chair, then traipsing all the way around the table, he advanced closer to Samuels. As the admiral pushed his chair away from the table, Rodríguez leaned forward and placed his hands on its armrests and brought his face within a few centimeters of the admiral's. Speaking, hardly above a whisper, he hissed, "Obey my orders, Admiral, or I swear, I will report your disloyal treasonous words to President Victor."

The admiral remained seated with fierce hostile eyes, until finally, a sense of wariness prevailed, and reluctantly, he said, "Aye aye, sir."

However, even as he executed this deception, Rodríguez was troubled. He questioned whether he was simply doing his duty as a soldier...or instead doing something dishonorable.

In truth, when he compared himself to Hawkins, he suffered from a tortured paradox. His inner desire to be noble, selfless, and virtuous competed with his profoundly base and self-promoting nature.

29

ALL IN

The bridge of the *Indefatigable* was cold and inhospitable. Hawkins shivered, but not from the cold. The capture and mistreatment of so many colonists and rebels was a terrible wound to him, but the most painful of all, was news that both Alyssa and Joshua were captives on Zeno under the cruel domination of Warden Seward.

He raged against Charles Victor, against Jacob Seward, against everything they stood for, and everything that now stood in his way. It filled him with a great twisted fury that wrung, exhausted, and drained his being—turning his flesh and blood into icy resolve.

He knew instinctively . . .

Rage is a destructive emotion.

And yet, he was alive with that overwhelming dark passion—an emotional firestorm dominating his mind and reason. He knew only one purpose—to rescue those taken.

Under his command, the ships *Indefatigable, Castor, Retribution,* and *Liberty* headed to Zeno. The bridge crew of the *Indefatigable* exchanged concerned furtive glances, but there was no hesitation in their performance.

The planet had plenty of time to scan the ships as they approached and its fortress was primed when they reached high orbit. The fortress opened fire first and splashed radiation on the shields of the rebel fleet.

The weapons officer reported, "We're within weapon's range, Captain."

"Commence firing."

Hawkins concentrated gun and missile fire on the fortress to suppress its heavy weapons. After an hour of heavy bombardment, the fort was weakening and Hawkins ordered his ships into a lower orbit so *Liberty* could begin unloading its five hundred soldiers stashed in its cargo compartments. Its shuttles dove to the planet's surface under the covering fire from the rebel fleet.

Several shuttles exploded, but most arrived safely and disgorged their troops with Hale leading the landing force while Hawkins remained on the *Indefatigable.*

Hale said, "I hope we survive this. Good luck."

Hawkins said, "Survival is what you have to do after things go wrong. I hope I've planned better than that. Remember speed is everything. It's all a matter of time. We don't have much. I'll cover the landing as long as I can, but you must move quickly, or we'll fail."

A million kilometers away, aboard the Special Forces flagship, *Ajax,* Rodríguez timed his countermove perfectly. The Special Forces Fleet came out of stealth mode and drove at full speed toward Zeno.

Alarms sounded throughout the rebel task force as the Jaxon force approached. The ships took only seconds to reach their highest level of readiness.

Aboard the *Indefatigable,* Hawkins waited patiently in orbit, ready to direct the rebel fleet's defense.

The *Ajax* along with three frigates and six sloops charged headlong at the *Indefatigable* and her consort.

It's wasn't a good policy to open fire at maximum range. The first salvo, patiently calculated and properly aimed, was too precious an opportunity to use lightly. It needed to be optimized for best effect. Hawkins selected an individual target and ordered the first broadside salvo to fire at optimal range with great precision at the lead Jaxon frigate, significantly damaging it. The ship fell out of formation and limped out of the battle.

"Grand shooting! Grand!" boomed Gunny's baritone voice.

Hawkins's heart beat rapidly as he realized that his efforts had paid off. He wanted to leave orbit, but he had to remain to cover the landing force.

A second coordinated rebel broadside knocked another Jaxon ship out of action. The rebels now had a fair chance in a toe-to-toe slugging match with the remaining Jaxon ships. However, the enemy was known to be resourceful.

The battle was now violently joined as the *Ajax* fleet altered their course to fire their broadsides.

The Jaxon ships managed a ragged barrage which wasn't as destructive they had hoped, but nevertheless, damaged the *Retribution* and the *Liberty*.

But as it turned out, the rebels still had a great deal of fight left in them. They fired another coordinated broadside at the *Ajax*.

As a sloop maneuvered to shield the *Ajax*, she exploded in a fiery ball and disappeared.

The Special Forces Fleet closed on the rebels.

Hawkins ordered the *Indefatigable* to fire as rapidly as possible. He left the *Castor* to cover the landing site while the *Indefatigable* and *Retribution* accelerated toward the enemy.

The engagement remained brutally violent as they closed.

The *Ajax* task force fired another salvo. It crippled the already damaged *Retribution*.

Gunny reported, "*Retribution* is a wreck, barely able to navigate, let alone defend herself."

The enemy frigates launched another devastating salvo at the fragile converted cargo ship, the *Liberty*. She suffered more and more damage until her captain was forced to abandon ship.

The *Indefatigable* was now a shadow of her former self. The harmony that typified a well-coordinated, finely-tuned machine had dissolved. Her engines weren't in their normal rhythm; the ship's motion was slightly erratic, though

Hawkins couldn't put a name on the difference. He sensed the ship and its crew were hurting.

He ordered, "Helm, intercept the nearest enemy."

"Aye, Captain."

With the enemy now closing on the *Indefatigable*, they came around and headed directly toward the *Ajax*.

"Mmmm," said Hawkins watching the enemy bear down on him. A wave of apprehension and excitement didn't stop him from calculating his next course of action. He swallowed hard and set his plan of action in motion.

Because the *Retribution* was no longer able to respond to communications, he coordinated his ship's fire with the *Castor*. He managed to concentrate their fire at the foe.

All ships reloaded their weapons. The *Retribution* remained on the starboard side of the *Castor* in an attempt to find shelter. The devastating accuracy of the Jaxon ships was disheartening. Each side approached unwaveringly.

Hawkins wrenched his mind away from the turmoil and forced himself to concentrate on his next action. He ordered his ship to maneuver to better support the damaged ships and still cover the landing site.

As the battle ebbed and flowed, the enemy ships drew ever closer and more threatening. The ship-to-ship battle was only one hour old and many had already died.

The *Indefatigable's* position was in a lower orbit than that of an enemy frigate. She was engaging closely, but was taking a terrible pounding. To her credit she was beating up on the enemy too.

The enemy fire contributed to the confusion around the *Indefatigable*.

"Damn them! Damn them all!" Gunny's baritone voice could be heard on the bridge over the din of confusion.

The enemy came on in an attempt to finish the fight. A word from Hawkins swung the *Indefatigable* toward the nearest enemy ship. The ships were now fighting in the clinches.

Gunny said, "Their fire is slackening. I'm sure of it."

They passed ahead of one frigate as it came up on their starboard quarter. The action commenced abreast until the enemy ship passed ahead. When he had gained sufficient distance, it raked them. Hawkins fumed; the *Indefatigable* was unable to bring a single weapon to bear upon the frigate.

The ship bore around upon her heel, and ran toward the *Ajax*. The ships were close and they used their secondary weapons to light up the enemy.

They separated momentarily and then the action recommenced, even more deadly than before. Nothing deterred them.

At that critical juncture, Hawkins ordered the *Castor* to launch an all-out counterattack by charging at the enemy ships. Despite this tactic, the enemy streamed forward. If anything the enemy ships continued with renewed ardor. Castor's attack led her to become the main target of the Jaxon fleet and after repeated close broadsides the ship was so severely holed, her crew had to abandon ship, adding a second rebel wreck in orbit.

Hawkins hoped the *Ajax* would stop to reorganize its task force. He tried to balance in his mind the calculus of ships lost on each side, to reach a conclusion that he could accept.

The weapons' fire from the *Indefatigable* was conducted with so much skill and effect that the enemy frigate finally turned aside.

The engagement between the two forces was hotly contested. The outcome hung by a thread. If it broke against Hawkins, all hope would be lost.

His limping ship circled around and prepared another attack. After exchanging several shots, the sloop veered away. She'd had enough. She was so badly damaged that she could no longer fight, but could only look for a means to escape certain doom. Hawkins maneuvered further away and started taking long range shots.

With all the rebels badly damaged, the *Indefatigable* was now essentially alone in a desperate battle with the remaining enemy frigates.

It was a difficult moment, but Hawkins had to make a decision and live with the consequences . . .

Courage will only get you so far.

The *Indefatigable* had sustained significant damage and a hull rupture had opened. Before the air became too thin, they had to isolate the leak. A column of smoke drifted across the compartment.

The smoke wafted through the corridors. A noxious fetid stink caused him to pull back from the fumes. Lights flashed critical information. The environmental systems were overloaded and failing.

Hawkins cursed.

He was merely following the only course available to keep his ship fighting.

Almost forgotten, the *Retribution* had been marked as dead long ago, but thanks to the cover the *Indefatigable* had afforded her, she was still intact, limping away from Zeno.

The severely damaged *Indefatigable* and the derelict *Retribution* were all that were left of the rebel force in the debris strewn space over the planet.

Though the rebels had inflicted massive damage to the Special Forces Fleet, it was still a strong and powerful force. Hawkins was out of options. To remain and fight against such prodigious odds would mean the senseless slaughter of his men. The frequent nearby explosions were enough to convince Hawkins that the remaining Jaxon frigates and sloops were too well led, and too dangerous, for him to remain over Zeno. He reluctantly ordered his crippled beaten ships away from the planet.

He stared in dismay at the naked landing site—the visible impoverished results of his error—an error that exposed a deep flaw in his thinking—an error that would propagate to the detriment of all who had followed him.

He watched from afar, as Rodríguez led a landing force of several hundred men to the surface, leaving Admiral Samuels in command of the Special Forces Fleet in orbit over Zeno.

Hale's five hundred soldiers on Zeno had initially made good progress against the poorly led troops of Seward. He captured the fort and reached the gates of the prison when he received the message from the *Indefatigable*.

In the bitterest moment of his life, a crestfallen Hawkins admitted, "I am unable to defend the landing site any longer. I'm taking what's left of the fleet to the other side of the planet. You can expect Rodríguez to start landing reinforcements behind you."

Hale's men were already being relentlessly pounded from space. Mortified, Hale could only respond, "An unhappy assessment."

Hawkins was sick at heart from his crushing failure. *All is lost.*

As night fell, Rodríguez faced great resistance on the ground from Hale's rebels. He sent a message to the *Ajax*, "Admiral Samuels, fire the fleet's heavy weapons directly into the prison compound. Start at the building's nearest the walls and destroy the entire surrounding palisades."

Samuels replied, "The detained amnesty colonists are still being held in cells within that compound."

"There are rebels dug in, and around, the bastions of the prison. They're putting up a stout defense. I have no choice. Now do as I ordered, and pour fire down on them," roared Rodríguez.

"That would be a war crime, to which, I will not be a party," responded Admiral Samuels with equal venom.

"Open fire immediately, or I'm have you court martialed in front of President Victor!"

Forced to make the toughest choice of his life, Admiral Samuels said, "Go ahead, do your damnedest. I don't care what you want anymore—I just don't damn well care." With that, he 'folded his hand,' and the ordered his battered fleet to leave.

Between fury and frustration, Rodríguez unleashed savage curses as the Special Forces Fleet left orbit and departed Zeno.

All is not lost!

Hawkins brought the remnants of the rebel fleet, back over the landing site. Even though they were badly damaged, the *Indefatigable* and the *Retribution* provided some meager cover fire as he gathered every man his ships could spare and landed them behind Rodríguez troops on the outskirts of the Zeno prison complex.

As the rebels began landing, several enemy cannons sent shells that exploded on the ground around them. Everyone was already exhausted; now cold windy dusty debris spewed directly into their faces. The earth shook and the sky was alive with the thunderclaps of more explosions. One struck so close to Hawkins that it knocked him flat on his back. His body became numb and his legs refused to obey his urgent pleading.

Move!

He couldn't remember what he had to do.

How long was I unconscious?

It had only been a few seconds, but he swung in and out of lucidity.

He was bleeding from shrapnel wounds. He cursed and screamed oaths into the darkness. Then he moved forward once more.

The rebels took cover momentarily until the barrage lifted, they swarmed forward again. An obstructing enemy strong point was eliminated and a key parapet was captured. Another parapet in the center of the position toppled over, completely blocking the way. Men began digging into the dry hard soil trying to construct some cover. Crawling on his belly, Hawkins crept forward with several men following him.

For a moment, Hawkins thought they had succeeded in reaching a good position, but he was wrong. The enemy was reorganizing and appeared as stronger than ever.

Rodríguez's men were entrenching to their rear, even as they continued to attack Hale's position which surrounded the prison defended by Seward. The layered battle continued in a confusion of ambiguous directions.

Hawkins sent a message to Hale telling him to hold out and that help was on the way. He added that he was going to lead a group through the maintenance tunnels into the inner prison control center. If possible, Hale was to meet him there when he won his way through.

With a final "Good luck," they signed off to deal with their respective battlefronts.

Hawkins ordered Gunny to continue to fight to reach Hale while he took twenty men through the maintenance tunnels. He followed the tunnels under the prison and worked his way toward the prison central control room. It took nearly an hour of treading their way through the tunnels and breaking through security hatches before Hawkins and his men reached the inner prison area.

When they reached the area under the security control center, they had to fight their way past a dozen guards until they controlled the cell locking mechanisms. Then they released the prisoners and sent them back through the tunnels toward the rebel lines.

Hawkins found Joshua among the prisoners. Joshua stayed with him while the other prisoners used the maintenance tunnels to escape.

After detailing the remainder of his men to escort the prisoners to safety, Hawkins and Joshua proceeded to look for Alyssa. Hawkins guessed that Rodríguez and Seward might be keeping her as a hostage somewhere near the warden's office.

As they approached the office, a red dot magically appears on Joshua's torso; Hawkins watched in slow-motion horror as a bright red flower blossomed and grew on the boy's chest until the pencil laser beam burst through his heart.

Joshua collapsed to the ground.

BANG! BANG! BANG!

Hawkins fired his pistol three times and dropped the assailant. To his surprise, it was his old tormentor, Lasseter—the vicious con whose gang had made his own stay on Zeno so hellish, so long ago. Knelling over Joshua, he picked up his head and cradled it in his arms. Joshua had trusted him to make everything good and right, but he had failed.

A consequence of my choices.

He listened to gun fire in the distance, but he couldn't pull himself away from the boy whose bravery had first inspired him to act at Newport, so very long ago.

Finally, Hawkins laid Joshua's body onto the ground and rose over him. He pulled his eyes away and began to walk toward the action. Soon, he was running, thinking of Alyssa, desperate not to fail her, too.

He came to the entrance of the warden's office where he expected to find Seward and his staff. They would know where Alyssa was.

He burst through the unlocked door.

Alyssa was tied to a chair at the far end of the room.

He only took two steps into the room before an alarm went off inside his head. Some fine nerve of remote perception warned him that he had, once again, charged into peril. Before he could heed that counsel—a red dot appeared on his chest.

He whipped around and fired at the source.

BANG! BANG! BANG!

Seward's frothing mouth spat out insults, but as he looked at his own chest, he trembled, and went white. Clutching his chest, he cried for mercy.

A moment later, he dropped to the ground—dead.

A fresh red dot lit up on Hawkins' chest.

He swung back around toward the new source and pressed the trigger—again, again, and again.

CLICK! CLICK! CLICK!

Empty.

He took a deep breath and waited for the red dot to turn into a pencil laser beam and penetrate his heart.

30

ONE MAN

Rodríguez had him. He knew he had him and the elation nearly suffocated him. He took several deep breaths to calm down. He considered Hawkins, considered the situation, and considered what he wanted. One thing he knew for certain was that his fury had finally led to victory, and he relished it. Now he needed to turn the fury into control.

He walked, forward one hand curled around his gun and the other bracing it underneath. His finger slipped from the trigger guard to the trigger. The slightest pressure and Hawkins would be dead, and there was nothing he could do—nothing but wait to die.

Though flushed with triumph, Rodríguez could not bring himself to the culminating act. The silence lingered, mysteriously binding the two men together, like oil mixing in water. It was strangely disconcerting. It filled him with an uncomfortable morbid curiosity.

He said, "This will make a fine story—in the retelling."

"Ha!"

"I'm glad you can find humor in it."

He's smug—arrogant—unyielding, thought Rodríguez

Seemingly without rancor, Hawkins asked, "What are your thoughts?"

"Now that the hunt is over, I find I have none," Rodríguez lied. "I've found you to be . . . very ordinary, when all this time . . . "

"What? You imagined someone larger than life?" asked Hawkins.

"Yes."

Again the silence stretched unbearably. They had nothing to say to each other, yet neither was willing to let the conversation die.

"Will you tell me why?" asked Rodríguez. He breathed evenly, in and out, through his nose with deliberation, trying to persuade the tension in his shoulders to melt away.

"Why what?"

"Why did you walk into this trap? You obviously knew from the outset that everything about Zeno was an elaborate trap, yet you dove in, as reckless as ever."

"As reckless as you expected?"

"Yes, just as I expected. But it still doesn't make sense to me."

"No, it wouldn't," said Hawkins. "Not to you."

Rodríguez was close to the edge. He had taken his own risks in his desperation to succeed. He thought he had won, but there was a nagging little tick in his brain, an old creeping fear that something was not quite right, something he perhaps should be worrying about, but had too easily dismissed.

He had gotten exactly what he wanted. Hadn't he?

His thoughts were interrupted by memories of the battle on Gambaro Ridge, where Hawkins had saved his life.

"I'm sorry."

Rodríguez said it without qualification, equivocation, sarcasm, or anything to mitigate its intent. The words sounded sincere, believable, like an act of contrition.

"I don't doubt you," said Hawkins.

With an off-handed shrug, Rodríguez said, "A soldier obeys orders."

"All orders?"

Rodríguez frowned, a deep troubled frown, one that roiled in the hurt it hid. He opened his mouth slightly, as if he were about to speak, but couldn't find the words.

"It's not enough to have the courage to fight," said Hawkins. His eyes were unreadable. "You have to fight for what's right."

"Do you alone know what's right?" demanded Rodríguez.

"Every man must discover for himself—if he's a man of honor."

That was the last thing Rodríguez had expected to hear. A blow to the face would not have had a greater impact. He snarled, "You insult me! Any other time I would not endure such abuse, but I will consider your statement an unfortunate consequence of your imminent demise."

Hawkins' brilliant sapphire eyes blazed as his gaze darted to a dark corner of the room. "Oh, but that may be merely a matter of timing," he said with a twinkle. "You see, I've saved you the unfortunate experience of falling into rough rebel hands. Instead, you're in my generous custody. Rest assured I shall be merciful."

Tightening his grip on the gun, Rodríguez said, "You misstate the obvious. I'm the one with the gun."

He said it with finality.

"Ha!" laughed Hawkins. Then leaning forward and speaking softly to draw all of Rodríguez's attention, he said, "Anthony, did you know that the most dangerous moments in battle are those that happen when you think it's over? When you think you've won and you're safe. When all of a sudden . . ."

WHAP!

With all her might, Alyssa struck Rodríguez from behind.

It was just a glancing blow, but everything happened too fast for Rodríguez to transition from a comfortable sense of power and control—to surprise—to anger—and then to—a physical response. His delayed reaction was slight, but enough to give Hawkins, his opportunity. He flung himself violently forward and grabbed Rodríguez's gun hand. His exceptional combat skills brought the clash to an instant conclusion.

Rodríguez lay unconscious on the ground.

"Jamie," said Alyssa, running to him.

Hawkins, finally admitted to himself, that he had loved her from the moment they'd met. He loved her even while they were separated by time and distance. Seeing her now brought it all back in a rush.

"It was a desperate struggle," said Alyssa, placing her hand on his chest, her eyes shining bright.

"A successful one—thanks to you," he said, drawing her closer.

He wrapped his arms around her. She nestled comfortably against his chest. Her sweet breath brushed against his cheek, and her soft hand caressed the nape of his neck.

After all the violence he had experienced, and the obstacles he had shattered to reach her, this moment was what he deeply desired.

They kissed—a deep passionate kiss.

BAM!

Together they jumped as the door slammed open against the wall.

Hale burst in.

He saw Rodríguez on the floor and Alyssa in Hawkins' arms.

Quietly, Hale said, "I guess the best man won."

-   The End   -

Are you curious about the unresolved alien signals in
Captain Hawkins?

Find the answer in the Sequel:

Coming soon

Captain Hawkins: The Greater Lie
by
H. Peter Alesso

Synopsis

Captain Jamie Hawkins and young Nathan McClain were
rebels fighting a corrupt Twenty-third Century government when they made a startling discovery—humanity
was not alone.

An ancient alien deep space signal planted a digital
seed into their world's computer networks. The seed grew,
evolved, and replicated into an adaptable artificial intelligence. The alien AI created false credentials allowing it
to gain control of elements of the government's security
force and military.

Fighting both the government and the AI, forced
Hawkins to take reckless risks as he went undercover to
penetrate the security apparatus suborned by the alien.
But before Hawkins could find a way to defeat the invader,
he learned that the alien had gained control of the planet's genetic engineering facility.

Why does an alien AI want the ability to alter human DNA?

Hawkins had to solve this alien logic puzzle.

The consequence of failure could mean the extinction of humanity.

FROM THE AUTHOR

I hope you enjoyed this book. I must confess—I'm proud of my characters and the story they tell. Hawkins and Alyssa are bold, brave, and possess a sense of humor. Their story is rich with a sense of personal responsibility and honor—qualities I admire.

I invite you to make a comment, suggestion, or speculation about alien life elsewhere in our Galaxy by posting a 5-Star review for *Captain Hawkins* on Amazon. I look forward to your ideas and criticisms which will encourage me to work harder on the next book.

In gratitude,
H. Peter Alesso
www.hpeteralesso.com

For notification of future books click the Follow button on the author page. Amazon Author: H. Peter Alesso

Made in the USA
Middletown, DE
14 January 2017